She was mesmerized by Juan's dark gaze

"Tell me," he murmured, "is your interest in me confined to Sa Virgen?"

"I—I don't understand," she stammered.

"I think you do." His fingers trailed down her sides, spreading to encircle her slim waist. "When I first saw you on Sa Virgen, you looked like some wild thing that belonged on the island. I had the strangest feeling..."

"What?" she whispered, as his voice trailed off.

"That *you*, not I, owned Sa Virgen. That I was the trespasser, not you."

Paula looked up at him in bewilderment. "But I was rude. You must have thought me a savage."

"I thought you... *guapissima*," he said.

Paula's heart thudded. He thought her beautiful. And she was alarmed at the intensity of the desire that suddenly filled her.

MADELEINE KER is a self-described "compulsive writer." In fact, Madeleine has been known to deliver six romances in less than a year. She is married and lives in Spain.

Books by Madeleine Ker

HARLEQUIN PRESENTS

HARLEQUIN ROMANCE

MADELEINE KER

KER

---

stormy attraction

Harlequin Books

TORONTO • NEW YORK • LONDON
AMSTERDAM • PARIS • SYDNEY • HAMBURG
STOCKHOLM • ATHENS • TOKYO • MILAN

Harlequin Presents first edition July 1989
ISBN 0-373-11185-1

Original hardcover edition published in 1988
by Mills & Boon Limited

CHAPTER ONE

DESPITE its being only the first week in March, Paula decided to risk the fangs of Cala Vibora.

The decision was made as soon as she saw the other boats moored at Cala Lom, the bigger, and much safer bay on the islet.

Sa Virgen was a popular haunt with yachtsmen from Majorca or the other islands. Given the spring sunshine, it wasn't surprising that others had ventured out from Palma this Saturday morning, giving their sails an airing on the first fine day of the year.

But Paula had suffered from an aversion to crowds all her life—an aversion she knew it was difficult to afford when you lived in a place like Majorca; but it was something intricately bound up with her love of nature, which was deep and strong enough to amount to a passion.

And when you saw what people did to the world around them, polluting the water and poisoning the air, there were times when you wanted to get as far away from humankind as possible! Love of clean air had made Paula Castle the sort of person to whom three boats in a bay constituted a crowd.

So she turned about, the little yacht slicing through the blue water, and steered a course for Cala Vibora.

She was not without some misgiving. 'Fangs' was no exaggeration. Like the viper it was named after, Cala Vibora possessed fearsome teeth of needle-sharp rock, gaping ominously out to sea. With its spectacular cliffs and treacherous currents, it wasn't ever a safe bay, especially not so early in the year. At the best of times it was a watery minefield of submerged rocks, which had claimed more than one careless sailor's life. But the payoff was a sheltered, golden beach that was almost never visited, and a chance of seeing some of the shyer animals of the Balearic islands, like giant turtles and the rapidly disappearing Eleonora's falcon.

'Besides,' she argued with her more cautious self aloud, 'it's so calm.'

Paula had got into the habit of reasoning with herself aloud as a teenager, and somehow had reached twenty-three without shedding the habit.

'It's almost like summer.'

Which was true. But for the cold breeze, which kept her in her oilskins, it would have been warm. A mile or two away, the coastline of Majorca was crystal-clear under a blue heaven. For the next twenty minutes, as she navigated round the headland to Cala Vibora, she enjoyed the sparkly feel of spring in the air.

As she guided the yacht into the jaws of Cala Vibora, Paula's face took on an expression of fierce concentration. Today, the bright reflection of the sea had given her eyes an intense green light, a colour they normally achieved only when she was furiously angry. Under normal circumstances, the eyes were a much warmer hazel, and formed one of the finest features of a very fine face.

The wind whipped masses of heavy chestnut hair across her full mouth and pointed chin, and she shook it away impatiently. This summer, she vowed with the part of her mind that wasn't sailing the boat, she would get these heavy tresses cropped, and to hell with whatever Daddy might say.

It required judgement to set a course between the angle of the wind and swell of the current. She felt the quivering vibration of the keel, rising up into the teak deck, transmitting itself through the rubber soles of her shoes. Maybe this hadn't been such a good idea, after all.

For an awful moment she felt she was going to slam the boat into a humped mass of evil-looking rock; fear was a physical pain in her chest and stomach. Then she was slipping by with a yard to spare, and gliding into the still, turquoise waters of the bay, unscathed by the viper's bite.

Relief and delight made her eyes sparkle as she hauled the sail down, her lithe body moving with the fluidity of long experience. It was as still as a pond within the bay, and she gave a sigh of contentment. It had been worth the effort in the end. Absolute peace...

She pulled on the tiller to steer the still-gliding boat towards the crescent of white sand that nestled in the embrace of the wooded sandstone cliffs.

Which was when she saw the motor-launch, moored in the shallows.

'Of all the...oh, *damn*!'

She couldn't help the exclamation of disgust that rose to her lips. All that risk and trouble, just to have the place to herself, and once again she'd been beaten to it!

She eyed the other boat grimly. In Paula's mind, boats fell into two categories—the serious and the frivolous. Without any very good reason, she automatically placed the family's yacht in the first category. Whereas this other boat very definitely belonged in the second.

It wasn't white, like every other boat in the harbour, but the charcoal grey of a shark. Long and low, it reeked of speed, power and money. Especially money. The massive engines alone—twin turbodiesels, if that kind

of thing turned you on—which now hung poised idly
over the stern would have cost as much as the yacht she
was sitting on. The rest of it looked sleek and mean.
Shaped not to float tolerantly on the water, but to thrust
ruthlessly through any kind of sea. And it had thrust its
way in here before her.

Paula stared at it in irritation for a long while, the
tiller slack under her arm. Somehow, the spring sky
seemed less blue, the day less balmy.

Finally she gave a mental shrug. It would be stupid
to let herself be turned away again. She could tolerate
a few members of the jacuzzi-and-tonic set. At least they
weren't roaring round the bay at full throttle, or setting
up a barbecue on the beach. She possibly wouldn't even
catch a glimpse of them.

She dropped anchor and stripped off the bulky oilskins. Any male eyes that might have been watching
would have widened appreciatively at that point, because Paula Castle had a superb figure. The tight red
sweater and denim Levis did nothing to hide the taut
curves that had been fashioned by a combination of
heredity—Paula's mother still turned heads wherever she
went—and long summers of energetic sailing.

There was also the way she moved. A boyfriend once
described it as like a Persian cat stalking; and indeed,
there was a fluid grace about her movements around the
yacht that made her worth watching. Not a move seemed
out of place as she lowered herself easily into the rubber
dinghy, and paddled towards the beach.

Her hair was that rich, dark colour, with coppery
glints, which is usually called 'chestnut' for want of a
better word. Its dense, curly waves framed a face which,
according to her father, was too wide for true beauty.
Her cheekbones were certainly full and high, tapering

to a neat chin that framed a luscious, mobile mouth. But Paula's mother, not as decisive as her husband on the question of Paula's lack of true beauty, had observed merely that there was no shortage of young men to crowd the house out at weekends, jostling for attention from those big hazel eyes...

The charcoal-grey launch was even bigger and sleeker from the dinghy, a symphony of anodized alloy and smoked glass. There seemed to be no one aboard. As she passed by, she read the name *Epoca* on the sharply raked prow. She didn't remember having seen her in the marina, but there were so many yachts moored in Palma harbour that it was hard to keep track.

In the lapping shallows she waded ashore, her rolled-up jeans revealing beautiful calves that still wore last year's tan, only slightly paled by the short Majorcan winter. Still, it felt like a long time since she'd been to Sa Virgen. As she put her shoes back on, she let the peace of the island seep back into her.

But for the mewing of gulls and the murmur of the sea, it was as tranquil as the first day of creation. High above her, scarcely seeming to move, two falcons hung against the blue sky.

The oilskin pouch that she wore slung round her neck contained a small but powerful pair of binoculars. She focused on the drifting falcons. A male and a female, fierce yellow eyes raking the island for mice, or the lizards Majorcans called *dragons*. Somewhere along the rocky crags, there would be chicks in a nest.

The thought made her smile with pleasure. Sa Virgen was thickly wooded enough to be the last refuge of some of the rarest species in the Mediterranean. Apart from a very rough and squiggly road, rising aimlessly up to Puig Virgen, the highest point, the island bore almost no marks of man. In fact, 'Sa Virgen' meant 'the virgin' in Majorcan dialect, and the name captured both the unspoiled beauty and the vulnerability of the island.

Vulnerability, because even here the bulldozers threatened. For the past three years the island had been in the shadow of plans to turn it into a holiday centre for rich visitors—with a heliport and a marina and a luxurious holiday village of a hundred and fifty apartments, just for starters.

The idea was so obscene as to make her wince. Why were people so greedy? Why couldn't they see what would be lost when Sa Virgen was finally violated?

From this vantage-point she had a good view of the luxurious interior of the motor-launch. The line of her mouth pursed in a mixture of disapproval and envy. It was more like a New York penthouse than a yacht. Wool carpets and grey leather everywhere, making no concession whatsoever to shipboard life. The cabins under that sleek deck would no doubt be equally amazing.

She could see a bowl of tropical fruit on a table on the afterdeck. Also, with widening eyes, a bottle of champagne cooling in an ice-bucket. Good God! If she stayed here long enough, she might see more than she wanted to!

Pity she couldn't take a five-minute stroll around that immaculate deck... It would at least be a story to tell her brother James, who was back from London for a six-week holiday, and who adored boats even more than she did. There was something guilty yet pleasurable about this kind of peeping! She could see into the cockpit, where a complex bank of instruments gleamed around the brass wheel. Slung carelessly across one of the seats was what looked like a woman's coat. Propping herself up on her elbows, Paula focused carefully on the clothes, intrigued.

And jumped in shock as the deep voice came from behind her.

'Sulky Susan—I presume?'

Paula rolled round in one fluid movement, the binoculars dangling loose round her neck. She hadn't heard the approaching footsteps, had been too intent on——

She flushed crimson as she realised just what she had been intent on.

There were two figures standing over her, a man and a woman. It was the man who had spoken, and who was smiling gently. The woman was not.

'I—I beg your pardon?' Paula stammered.

'You must be Sulky Susan.' The man nodded his dark head casually in the direction of the bay. 'That's the name of your boat, isn't it?'

'Oh—y-yes.' He must have eyes like a hawk to spot the *Sulky Susan* name-plate from up here. Hot with embarrassment, Paula rose to her feet and faced them.

The woman, though unusually fair-skinned, had pitch-black hair and eyes. She was very beautiful in a way that was both cool and yet passionate. The perfection of her features was set off by an almost animal quality at the eyes and nose. At this moment she was wearing an expression of disdain which sat on them particularly well. There could hardly have been a greater contrast between her unruffled elegance and Paula's own *déshabilé*. Her cream wool cape was exquisite, a garment of high fashion, rather than utility. Like her beautiful wool skirt and shoes, it proclaimed wealth and style well out of the common run.

The man, who was dark, and unmistakably Spanish, was very tall. Obviously in the prime of his life, Paula guessed him to be about thirty-five or -six. He had the kind of male figure that made any clothing look fabulous. His dark grey cashmere jersey, to match the launch, no doubt, moulded itself to a lean, lithe-waisted torso with broad, muscular shoulders. Like Paula herself, he wore denims that were tight enough to reveal the hard strength of lean hips and long, sinewy thighs. From the knees down, his legs were encased in slick waterproof boots, the sort that cost their weight in gold.

That these two were the champagne-drinking owners of *Epoca* would have been in no doubt had there been a dozen yachts in the bay below.

The woman turned to her companion, and said in very aristocratic Castilian Spanish, 'Who is she? What was she looking at?'

Paula brushed fragments of thyme off her jersey irritably. 'My name is Paula Castle,' she said. It was so embarrassing to have been caught peeping at these people's boat that she felt she had to offer some kind of explanation. She went on in the best Spanish she could muster—which was easily as good as the raven-haired woman's—'I was watching the gulls along the cliff. I didn't intend to spy on your boat.'

'My dear Miss Castle,' the man said easily, in English, 'nobody would dream of such an accusation.'

There was something wickedly mocking about that purring voice. Paula glanced at him in annoyance.

And on closer inspection, he was by far the more remarkable of the two. Where the woman's beauty had a cool, porcelain quality that might have come off any fashion magazine cover, the man's face was unforgettable.

To start with, his eyes and mouth held a brooding sexuality that was heart-stopping. Their smile expressed supreme confidence in his own manhood, in his power over woman.

The eyes, like the thickly arching brows and the dense, rather curly hair, were black. Lines of experience at temple and jaw added authority; but it was the nose that added the final, almost shocking touch. Once noble, it had been badly broken some time in the past, and the resetting had left a crooked kink in the formerly straight lines.

The result was a mixture of beauty and brutality that was utterly disconcerting, and, as Paula looked into the smoky black eyes, she felt a sudden weakness at the knees.

He was devastating! In the depths beyond that smile there was something else, something darker and much more primitive. Astonished at the response in her own body, Paula felt the shiver ripple up her spine, spreading ghostly fingers across her breasts and stomach.

As though she sensed the *frisson* that went through Paula at that moment, the woman made an impatient noise under her breath. The subtle smile on the man's deeply chiselled mouth widened.

'You must be a brave girl,' he said gently. 'You took quite a risk coming through Cala Vibora.'

'No more than you took,' Paula retorted, not liking that 'girl'—especially not from this man.

'That is not true.' The deep intonation was characteristically Spanish, and his English was formal, but almost perfect. 'We have five-hundred-horsepower engines to take us through the current. You depend on the wind—which is fickle. You were sailing very close to the rock.' A slight movement of his head indicated the route she'd taken in. 'We watched you.'

Paula hid her discomfort. So they'd watched her from the time she'd arrived, had seen her toddle up the cliff like a bug across a cabbage, flop down on the grass and start peering at their launch. 'I come here often—to look at the birds,' she said tersely, still speaking Spanish. 'I know exactly what I'm doing.'

'Indeed?' He raised one eyebrow, as though deeply impressed. It was the kind of teasing that Paula most detested.

'Indeed,' she said shortly. 'And now, I'm sorry to have disturbed you, so I'll just keep going along the cliff.'

'Not that way.' The effortless command in his voice stopped her retreat in its tracks. 'The path has collapsed during the recent rains. There's no way forward.'

Paula hesitated, mistrustful. It *had* been raining hard recently; walls and even roads had collapsed on Majorca.

'We've just come back,' he went on, apparently amused that she should doubt his word. 'It's very dangerous. I wouldn't consider letting you go up there.'

She gave him a dry look, irritated by his proprietorial tone.

'I speak your language perfectly well,' she said thinly in Spanish. 'Quite as well as you speak English, in fact. You don't need to patronise me.'

'Very well,' he replied in the same language, and gave her the ghost of a smile. 'We'll pander to your linguistic vanity instead of mine.'

The woman had been silent up till now. Her dark eyes had turned from Paula to the man in turn, her expression cold. Now she said in a tone of some impatience, 'Come, Juan. Let's go.' Even more drily, Paula remembered that the champagne—and no doubt other delights—were waiting on board *Epoca*.

'But I am intrigued,' he said, never taking his eyes off Paula, 'by this Paula Castle, who sails through Cala Vibora to look at birds, and who knows exactly what she is doing. Besides, we have not introduced ourselves yet. Miss Castle, may I introduce you to my companion, Cristina Colom? Cristina, meet Paula Castle. Though I feel that Sulky Susan suits her rather better. And my name is Juan Torres.'

He was holding out his hand to her, and she had little choice but to give him her own. He raised it to his lips with a slight bow, and touched her knuckles with warm lips.

Paula felt the blood rise to her cheeks. And at that moment, the woman who had just been introduced as Cristina Colom burst into laughter.

It was genuine, not affected amusement. With an almost physical sense of pain, Paula realised how ridiculous she must appear—a tousled tomboy in jeans and a thick jumper, dazedly watching while this supremely attractive man mockingly kissed her hand. The sort of joke a renaissance nobleman might enjoy playing on a milkmaid.

She snatched her fingers away, her face tightening. Paula didn't like being the butt of anyone's jokes. Especially not when they were hurtful jokes. 'What is so amusing?' she enquired tautly.

'Your expression,' the woman said maliciously. 'You obviously aren't used to having your hand kissed.'

If Juan Torres shared her amusement, he was hiding it better. 'My manners are absurdly old-fashioned,' he dismissed the moment with a slight shrug. As though noting the angry flush still in her cheeks, he looked directly into her eyes, and added softly, 'It was not my intention to insult you, Paula.'

'I'm not in the slightest insulted,' Paula retorted stiffly. She pulled her jersey straight with a quick movement that brought her breasts into momentary relief against the soft wool. His smoky gaze did not miss the fact.

Nor did he make any attempt to hide his interest in the rest of her body, his eyes assessing the shape of her figure beneath the tight jeans, then lifting to examine her face. She tried to answer the inquisitive stare, but it was too bold. It held a challenge, a statement of desire, which she couldn't meet. With a strange fluttering in her stomach, Paula looked away.

'Tell me,' he asked, 'how often to you come to Sa Virgen?'

'As often as I feel like,' she replied coldly.

'As often as *you* feel like?' the other woman snorted in amusement at Paula's tone. 'You talk as though you, and not he, owned the island!'

Owned? Paula looked at the man sharply. *Juan Torres.* The name hadn't registered at first, but now she felt her heart give a sudden lurch. She, who was such an expert on Sa Virgen, hadn't even known who she was talking to.

Because if this man *was* Juan Torres, then he was indeed the owner of Sa Virgen. And he was also the man behind Proyecto Virgen SA, the company whose plans to urbanise the island had aroused such fury in Paula's heart, not to mention a lot of other hearts!

'You are *the* Juan Torres?' She took a deep breath, feeling nervous anger flood her veins. 'Well, well! You must forgive me for not realising what a rare honour this is.' She let the acid drip into her voice. 'You seem to be a very shy man, Señor Torres.'

'A very private man,' he corrected her, unperturbed. 'Which is not the same as a shy man.'

'You don't like public appearances, at any rate.'

He surveyed her calmly. 'What makes you say that?'

'I've lost track of the number of debates there have been about Sa Virgen,' she replied. 'Debates about your plans for Sa Virgen, I mean. But you were specifically invited to all of them—and you didn't put in an appearance at a single one!'

'Ahh!' It was the woman who made the sound of comprehension. Her eyes were narrowed now. 'You're one of that gang of vandals and fanatics who've been causing so much trouble!'

'I'm a conservationist, not a fanatic,' Paula retorted indignantly. 'And I'd say that the vandalism was on Señor Torres' side, wouldn't you?'

'Not all of it, at any rate,' Juan Torres said with a spark of anger in his eyes. 'A group of people who called themselves conservationists chose to hold a demonstration on this island last summer. They did more damage to the ecology of Sa Virgen than anything in the past thousand years.'

'They got carried away.' But Paula was flushing. She'd always been grateful that she hadn't been part of that ridiculous and disgraceful episode. The trouble with causes like Sa Virgen was that they attracted a lunatic fringe who were all too eager to get completely out of hand. The 'Hands off Sa Virgen' episode had been an unmitigated disaster.

'Carried away?' the man said ironically. 'They started fires, left filth everywhere, screamed and shouted like savages. I can assure you that it was not an impressive sight, Miss Castle. There was very little love of nature in evidence.'

'They were disgusting,' the woman echoed.

'Their bad behaviour was nothing compared to what *you* intend to do to Sa Virgen,' Paula retorted. She glared at Juan Torres, hazel eyes a cold green. 'I happen to think that your plans for this island are completely obscene!'

'I gathered as much.' The sarcasm was so fine as to be almost intangible. 'May I ask what gives you the right to lecture me on my own island, Paula Castle?'

'Because you won't come and face your critics,' she accused him directly. 'You hide behind lawyers and spokesmen, people who make sure you never hear our arguments.'

'I hear them perfectly well,' he contradicted her, evidently growing impatient at her attack. 'I do, after all, read the newspapers. As to the debates you mentioned——' The merest lift of one eyebrow expressed a wealth of disdain. 'What would be the point of my presence? Simply to be abused and insulted by the ignorant?'

'*Ignorant* is not an appropriate word.' Now Paula was icy. The fact that he was at least ten years older than her, and a man of wealth and authority, didn't abate her anger in the slightest. 'The people who oppose the urbanisation of Sa Virgen include some of the foremost ornithologists and scientists in the Mediterranean. And for you to dismiss their learning so lightly reflects badly on *you*, Señor Torres, not on them!'

'In any case,' he went on with complete indifference to her eloquence, 'Sa Virgen belongs to me. Why should I consult anyone about my own intentions for my own property?'

The arrogance of it took Paula's breath away for a moment. 'You're not God, you know,' she told him rudely.

'Nor are *you*,' he retorted, eyebrows descending like thunderclouds.

'Why do you put up with this insolence?' Cristina Colom snapped to Torres. 'This girl is not worth arguing with, Juan. She isn't even a Spaniard. Why waste your breath?'

His angry expression eased. 'She shows a glimmering of intelligence,' he said with a slight smile, 'though I agree her manners are poor.' His eyes were still on Paula, eyes that were far too dark and intelligent for comfort. 'You speak excellent Spanish, Paula. I take it you are Tom Castle's daughter?'

'Yes,' Paula said, disconcerted and not altogether pleased. 'How did you know?'

'Your father is a successful novelist,' he replied. 'Most people on Majorca have heard of him. Does your father know that you've come out to Cala Vibora this morning?'

'I take the yacht out whenever I want to,' Paula replied defensively, sensitive to the implied criticism. 'My family don't worry about me. I've already told you, I come here often.' She tilted her chestnut head on one side, challenging him with her eyes. 'I assume you're going to throw me off your property now?'

'Not at all.' He was as smooth as velvet. 'I welcome visitors to Sa Virgen—especially if they respect the wildlife.'

The hypocrisy made her smile mirthlessly. 'And the helicopters that are going to bring in your well-heeled, "nature-loving" guests to their concrete apartments— are they going to respect the wildlife, too?'

'More than your so-called conservationists, at any rate,' he rasped. He was obviously annoyed at the way

Paula kept rejecting his attempts to smooth over the argument.

'Come on, Juan,' Cristina Colom said pointedly. 'Leave this madwoman here, and let's get back to the yacht.'

But Paula, once launched on a theme, was not that easy to shrug off. She'd never have forgiven herself for not speaking out when she had the unique chance of addressing Juan Torres personally!

Without taking her eyes away from Torres', she went on, 'How long do you think falcons can compete with helicopters and Land Rovers? You must know that this island is the last refuge of the giant turtles! Have you considered what will happen when hordes of ignorant people flood the beaches, digging up their eggs and taking them back to Boston and Manchester and Oslo as souvenirs?'

'Miss Castle——'

'Don't you *feel* anything for this island and its people?' she demanded fiercely. 'If you're the owner of Sa Virgen, then isn't your duty to protect her—and not to rape her?'

'Watch your tongue,' Torres snapped angrily.

'Does the word shock you?' Paula asked bitterly. 'It ought to. It's a shocking idea, Señor Torres. Just because you happen to have had enough money to buy yourself this island doesn't give you the right to despoil it!'

'Sa Virgen has belonged to the Torres family for a thousand years,' he flicked out, his face contemptuous. 'Since you're such an authority on Sa Virgen, I'm surprised you didn't know that.'

'My ancestry doesn't go that far back,' Paula snorted. These Spaniards and their family pride! 'In any case, that doesn't affect the main point. Building a holiday village on this island will mean the death of something unique. Something that will never be seen again.'

A bitter expression crossed Juan Torres' face. 'Earlier on, I thought you showed some signs of intelligence,' he said wearily. 'But these are the usual rantings of the pseudo-conservationist, Paula. You come to Sa Virgen yourself, as you say, whenever you feel like it. Yet you want to stop others from coming here. Is that not pure selfishness?'

'Others may not treat this place with the care I do!'

'And *that* is insufferable vanity of the very young.'

'I'm not too young to know right from wrong! In any case,' Paula said hotly, 'what I want to stop is any building on Sa Virgen, and anyone bringing machinery here—especially clattering helicopters, which will completely destroy the fragile ecosystem.'

'As a matter of fact,' he said curtly, 'helicopters were chosen precisely because they do not damage the ecosystem. Nor do the falcons, or any other fauna of this island, appear to mind the noise they make.'

'Oh, you've proved that, have you?'

'Yes, I have,' he rejoined coolly. 'And I intend to build the helicopter landing pad at the other end of the island, well away from the ecosystem of the falcons. When the holiday village is built, the helicopter will come to Sa Virgen only once a week.'

'Once a week? That's enough to disturb——'

'As for people invading the beaches to dig up turtle eggs,' he cut through, 'the idea is absurd. My guests on Sa Virgen will be people who love nature, and who have the means to afford what will be a very costly holiday. They will *not* be a destructive rabble.'

'Good God,' Paula said in amazement, shaking her head. 'You poor man! You actually believe that rich people care more about nature than poor people!'

His eyes narrowed, but he kept his temper. 'I believe that people who have paid a lot of money to enjoy an unspoiled island are less likely to damage it than people who trespass here uninvited.'

Something in the way he said it made Paula flush angrily. 'There are no signs forbidding ordinary people to come here. I suppose that will be the next thing?'

'I intend to make sure that the total number of people on the island is restricted,' he said bleakly. 'And that means keeping trespassers out, yes.'

'That's a dirty trick,' she exclaimed heatedly.

'It's necessary for the protection of the ecosystem you're so concerned about,' he clipped out.

Paula sneered. 'Well, thank heaven there are people who oppose you, and who care enough to do something.' Her eyes glittered dangerously. 'And it isn't *when* you build your holiday village, Señor Torres—it's *if* you build it.'

The impatient look on Torres' tanned, hook-nosed face was slowly replaced by one of interest. The interest of a tiger alerted by a lamb's bleat.

'Oh?' he purred. 'Is that a threat, Paula Castle?'

'You know as well as I do that there's considerable opposition to your plans,' Paula said grimly. 'In fact, there's a public debate about it in Palma, in a month's time. We're hoping to raise enough public concern to get your plans stopped. The Ministry of the Environment is sending a representative. And I know you've been invited, too,' she said pointedly. 'I hope I'll see you there.'

'Like the honourable minister of the environment,' he assured her forbiddingly, 'I'll certainly be represented.'

'Oh, I like that. *Represented*. By some lawyer? Some company man?' When Paula's eyes flashed scorn they could be very bright and hot indeed. 'Are you too cowardly to come in person?'

'You must be mad, girl.' Cristina Colom's expression was more amazed than angry. 'To talk to him like that——'

'Or is it the fact that, inwardly, you know that your own arguments are too feeble to bear scrutiny?' Paula pressed, ignoring the woman. 'Is that why you don't dare to air them in public?'

The glitter of dark light in Juan Torres' eyes might have been the turning of a blade in the sun. But by now he obviously had his own emotions under control, and he did not return her attack. It was hard to tell whether being attacked by this young and attractive stranger was annoying or amusing him. 'You may be a foolish and misguided young woman, but you have a way with words, Paula. In both English and Spanish.'

'And in German, French and Swedish,' she couldn't resist adding.

His face creased into a mocking smile, lips parting to reveal beautiful white teeth. 'Ah,' he said softly, 'thank God for a touch of vanity at last. I was beginning to wonder whether you were human after all.'

Bemused by the sheer attractiveness of his smile, Paula felt the anger drain out of her, like the wind dropping out of a full sail. Suddenly, she was shaking with a reaction of nerves, and the colour that had been so bright in her cheeks paled.

Without quite knowing how, she had run right out of steam, and now she was beginning to realise just how rude she had been to this rather awesome stranger—not to mention his lady-friend.

'Juan, we *must* go.' Cristina Colom's tone was dangerous. 'I know she's amusing and pretty, but you've wasted enough time with her. Shall we leave?'

For a second longer, his eyes held Paula's. Had he been ten years younger, and one of the boys who crowded round her at weekends, she might have been able to interpret what those coal-black eyes were saying. But he was very, very different from any of the men she knew, and Paula was at a complete loss to understand.

All she knew was that her stomach was aching with tension now, and that she'd have given a lot to be able to sit down and close her eyes.

'Of course, my love. Shall we walk back down?' With a formal gesture, he turned away from Paula, and guided the two women on to the rocky little path.

Paula had little choice but to go back with them the way she had come. She hadn't seen much wildlife, but she'd had a very remarkable visit, all the same...

Her knees almost too weak to support her, she found herself walking beside Torres, with Cristina's slim-legged figure a little way in front.

'Do give my regards to your father,' he was saying, his deep, rich voice as urbane as though they'd just been lunching in some restaurant, and not arguing fiercely on a wild cliff-top. 'I've enjoyed his books very much.'

'I'll tell him,' Paula muttered. This was conversation, not talk. The real interview was clearly at an end. Hard to believe it had ever happened. Wait until she told the Environmental Group that she'd actually met Torres, complete with sophisticated 'companion', on the cliffs of Sa Virgen!

He talked easily all the way back to the beach, the kind of smooth chat that didn't require more than monosyllabic answers from her.

Cristina Colom said nothing at all, and when they reached the golden sand, her aristocratic visage had lost any trace of emotion, unpleasant or otherwise. It was back to its initial mask-like beauty as she gave Paula a final glance.

'*Adios,*' she said coolly, the most final sort of greeting that can be given in Spanish. And though there had been no malice in either her face or her voice, Paula knew instinctively that she had made an enemy.

'Be careful going out through the rocks,' Juan Torres said seriously. 'Don't take it too fast. Understood?'

'Yes,' she mumbled, nodding. He walked her over to her dinghy, and helped her push it into the shallows.

Then, before she could object, or roll up her own jeans, he was lifting her into his arms as lightly as though she'd been a feather.

Nothing could have more sharply illustrated his power and her own insignificance! Clinging, red-faced, to the soft stuff of his jersey, Paula was agonisingly aware of hard, muscular arms around her hips and shoulders, of his male strength enfolding her.

Her body felt as hot as some wretched fish in a frying-pan as Torres waded into the water with her, and dumped her less than ceremoniously in the bobbing rubber cushion of the dinghy.

There was a wicked glint, rather than a smile in his eyes as he gave the dinghy a hard shove out towards the *Sulky Susan.*

'Come back whenever you feel like it,' were his parting words. 'There will be no signs to keep you out.'

Her skin burning where he'd touched her, Paula picked up the fibreglass oars, and started rowing out towards her yacht. Her heart was pounding as though she'd just run a mile, and every morsel of strength seemed to have left her arms. It was an effort to move. She'd have to settle herself down before she navigated those rocks!

Through the curly hair that blew across her face, she saw Torres' tall figure wading ashore towards Cristina. He gave no backward glance. What a man! The thought surfaced through all her embarrassment and righteous indignation against Juan Torres. She'd never met anyone remotely like him. Whatever the rights and wrongs of Sa Virgen, Juan Torres was a remarkable person, and a remarkably magnetic man. No one, enemy or friend, had ever had this kind of effect on her!

By the time she'd shipped the dinghy, and was hauling up *Sulky Susan*'s sails, she was feeling marginally more settled. Casting a glance across at the sleek grey shape of *Epoca*, she caught sight of Torres and Cristina on deck. Both were watching her, with no evident intention of leaving the bay themselves.

They were obviously waiting for her to leave them in privacy. Bitterly, it occurred to Paula that by the time she was out of Cala Vibora they would be making love in the cabins below. Or perhaps on the sunlit deck.

Gritting her teeth, she negotiated the mouth of the bay with as much aplomb as she could. She'd said she knew what she was doing, and by God, she'd better prove it now. Before she rounded the rocks that would take her out of sight, she shot one last look back. Torres was alone on the deck now. She saw his arm lift in a valediction that was probably more than half ironic. She gave the briefest of waves back, and unfurled the mainsail.

Then she was out of sight of the blue bay, and making her way back towards Palma.

CHAPTER TWO

'HE SAID he'd enjoyed my books?'

Tom Castle hacked at the Sunday joint in the barbarous way he'd always done, and looked pleased. 'I wonder whether he read them in English or in translation.'

'He didn't say.'

'It makes a big difference, you know. The jokes don't always come through...'

'Well, I only hope you didn't go over the top,' Paula's mother sighed. 'You're so intense about that wretched little island. And you should *never* have gone to Cala Vibora on your own! What exactly did you say to him?'

'I told him I thought his plans were obscene,' Paula recalled with relish.

'Oh, dear!'

'It's not a case of "oh, dear", mother,' James said with a grin. 'It's a case of well done, Paula. Having someone argue with him to his face must have been a novel experience for Don Juan Torres.'

'That's what I'm afraid of,' Margaret Castle said ruefully. 'Paula can be so *fierce* when she gets the bit between her teeth. The Spanish don't always understand.'

'I'm not sure I always understand myself,' Paula's father put in.

'Yes, well, she may have insulted the man. I'd hate to think that someone as important as Juan Torres was telling people that our Paula didn't have any manners.'

28

'Not too much gravy, Margaret. And from what I hear of Torres, it would take more than our Paula to make much of a dent in his armour.'

'True,' James smiled. 'He's a hard case. Though Mum's right; Paula can be very... what's the word I'm looking for, Dad?'

'Persuasive?'

'Exactly. Chewing the environment over at all those appallingly dull meetings has developed her arguing muscles to a high pitch. The impression Paula left on his mind is likely to have been a lasting one!'

'Someone has to care about the environment,' Paula said briskly, 'or pretty soon there won't be an environment left to care about.'

'Anyway,' James mused, 'I'd have given a lot to see that boat of his. Not to mention his female.'

'Glad you've got your priorities right,' his father smiled. James, who was almost five years older than Paula, was a doctor. Currently, he was working in London, but he came back to Majorca to visit the family as often as he could.

The house always seemed happier and noisier with him in it, and on this bright, clear Sunday afternoon, it was a very happy house. The only family member missing was Helen, who came between Paula and James in age. Of them all, Helen had melted most easily into the Spanish way of life. She'd married a Spaniard, and a year or two ago she'd gone to Barcelona with her husband, and was running a highly successful health-food shop there with him, leaving Paula as the last chick in the nest.

The Castle family had been in Majorca for a long time. Paula had been only seven when her father's first novel had been published in England. The money which that book had brought in had enabled him to give up his job as a maths teacher eighteen months later, and move to Majorca with his family.

They'd been living in this pretty villa ever since, with its peach-pink walls and tiled roof, just outside Palma. It was distinguished by three huge lemon trees in the garden. The golden fruits of the biggest were visible now, through the dining-room window.

While they weren't by any stretch of the imagination truly wealthy, Tom Castle's continuing success as a humorous writer had enabled the family to lead a happy, comfortable life in the sun.

As they ate their way through Sunday lunch, talking about Paula's passion for nature, the fate of Sa Virgen, and other matters, Paula had a vision of Juan Torres' dark, brutally handsome face at their table. He was so different from all of them. How on earth would they react to someone like Torres? Apart from Helen, they were all so distinctly English, and Torres was so—so alien.

He belonged to another world, of expensive boats and beautiful women. He owned an island. An *island*! God knew what else he owned. He must be enormously wealthy... Who was it had said the rich were different? Torres was certainly different. Yet it was more than nationality or wealth. It was a quality as different from James' happy-go-lucky altruism, or her father's wry humour, as brandy was different from wine.

'If he's rich enough to afford a luxury launch, and heaven knows what else,' Paula mused aloud, 'what does he need to exploit Sa Virgen for? He surely can't want the money...'

'As Wallis Simpson once said, you can never be too thin or too rich.' James smiled. 'Another million or two always comes in handy, you know.'

'If *I* owned Sa Virgen,' Paula declared, 'I'd never do anything to harm it—even if I was as poor as a church-mouse.'

'Funny,' James said. 'Our name is Castle—and *torres* means "towers" in Spanish. Not much chance of *détente* there, Paula. It sounds like a mediaeval battle. Don't fall in love with him; the omens aren't good.'

'I've no intention of falling in love with him,' Paula said airily.

'Then why have you never stopped talking about him for the past twenty-four hours?'

'He's a natural enemy. A despoiler of the environment.'

'Hmmm. You're rather susceptible to the dark, dangerous type, you know.'

James' teasing was irritating but amusing. As lunch came to an end, and they cleared the table, they were laughing happily at one another.

When the wreckage had been disposed of, Tom Castle, who was busy with a novel, disappeared in the direction of his study, while their mother made for the bedroom, and her Sunday afternoon siesta.

'What's on this afternoon?' her brother asked Paula. 'The usual parade of suitors coming round to moon over you?'

'Not that I know of. Why?'

'I thought we might go out in *Susan*.'

'Great!' Paula agreed, eyes glowing. 'Like old times?'

'On one condition.'

'What?'

'That we don't go anywhere near Sa Virgen,' he smiled. 'I'm on holiday, you know. Supposed to be resting. After that lunch, I'm not strong enough to face Cala Vibora— and *definitely* not strong enough to face Juan Torres!'

Memories of a whole weekend sailing were still vivid in her mind as she settled into the office the following week.

Paula had been with Gomila & Rodriguez for the past eighteen months, and she loved her work. Before that, she'd worked in a big estate agency for two and a half years. She'd finally left, disgusted by what she saw as the ruthless exploitation of the island's natural areas. In fact, it had been during those two and a half years, watching acres and acres of virgin, beautiful coastal landscape vanish under hotels, housing estates and concrete apartment blocks, that her sense of responsibility to the environment had crystallised into a passion.

As her love of the birds and plants of Majorca grew, Paula had started hating her work. When she'd read Gomila & Rodriguez's job advertisement in *Baleares*, she'd jumped at the chance.

She'd never regretted the move. Gomila & Rodriguez were one of the most important legal firms in Palma, and they worked her a lot harder than the estate agency had ever done, but they stretched her talents, and that was what she really enjoyed.

Paula's chief talent, as she'd boasted to Juan Torres on Saturday, was for languages. She and Helen had gone to an excellent school on the island. As well as learning Spanish and French at school, she'd taught herself to be fluent in Catalan, the distinctive Spanish spoken on Majorca. And during the time she'd spent at the estate agency, she'd taught herself both German and Swedish.

Languages just came naturally to her. She could slip from one into another with no confusion or hesitation, some miraculous switchboard in her brain taking care of all the potential crossed lines! At Gomila & Rodriguez she was rapidly becoming indispensable. The cosmopolitan population of Majorca brought a bewildering variety of problems to the office, and each day presented new challenges to meet, new areas to explore.

She was even considering taking some night-classes to improve her sketchy Italian, though she doubted whether her crowded life would stand much more scheduling...

There was, for example, her Environmental Group meetings, which she attended religiously on Wednesday evenings. Though the lectures and slideshows could sometimes be less than fascinating, the socialising afterwards brought her into contact with people, Majorcans and foreigners, who felt the same way she did, and who shared the same concerns about ecology.

When she arrived at the hall that Wednesday evening, there was a certain buzz of laughter in the air. As she gravitated towards the motley group of younger people who were her friends, she was aware of amused eyes glancing at her.

It was Gabriel Sanchez, occupying his usual place under the huge oil-painting of eagles on Puig Mayor, who enlightened her.

'Hello, there, Saint Georgina. Taken on any dragons lately? I hear you've been defending the honour of Sa Virgen singlehanded!'

Paula, used as she was to the speed with which all information circulated on Majorca, was amused rather than astounded. 'Now who told you that, Gabriel?'

'Everybody's telling everybody. It's common knowledge that you slapped Juan Torres' face on his own island——'

'What a fib!' she gasped. 'I never laid a finger on him!'

'—and that you told him in no uncertain terms what you thought of his holiday village and his heliport.'

'Now that I *did* do,' she admitted with a smile.

'Come on,' one of the girls urged, 'let's hear the official version.'

'Oh...it's so insignificant, really.'

'Nonsense! Tell all—unless you want the rumours to get *really* wild.'

Rather shamefacedly—the past few days had put her own behaviour into perspective—Paula gave them a brief account of what had happened on Saturday. The general reaction was one of delighted amusement. The fact that no one had hitherto succeeded in even meeting Juan Torres had elevated Paula's clash with the man to an almost legendary status. It was nice to be the centre of attention. The only thing that stopped her from completely blending into her role as heroine of the hour was that humiliating memory of being scooped up in those strong arms, and dumped in her dinghy, the way a fisherman would throw back a fish too small to eat.

She didn't tell them that bit.

'But how did he react to you?' The question, delivered with characteristic intensity, came from Barry Lear, the unspoken leader of the group. Barry was a tall, angular American, who worked at the Raptor Research Institute. He was one of the most dedicated conservationists on the island, and last year had given a memorable talk on the eagles of Sardinia and Majorca. 'I mean, how did he react to you *personally*?'

'Well...' Paula hesitated. 'I think he was rather amused, actually.'

'Amused?'

'His self-confidence is massive,' she explained. 'I felt like a bee trying to sting a man in armour. His lady-friend was a lot more annoyed with me than he was. Though at one point,' she remembered with a smile, 'I thought he was going to lose his temper.'

Barry cocked his head on one side. 'You got through to him?'

'He called me a pseudo-conservationist. And there was a look in his eyes...' She tailed off, quite unable to convey that alarming glitter in the black eyes of Juan Torres.

Barry Lear studied her for a moment. Like the birds of prey that were his passion, he had particularly keen, light brown eyes. He was in his early thirties, but so tanned and creased by sun and wind that he looked ten years older, an impression assisted by a rather grizzled blond beard. 'Do you think he took a fancy to you?' he enquired thoughtfully, aquiline features intent.

'Good lord, no!' But Paula was flushing slightly, maybe because it was the second time someone had made the same suggestion. Before anyone could pass any further comment, however, the guest speaker of the evening was being introduced, and the room darkened in preparation for the evening's slideshow.

The long and detailed lecture which ensued, about a group of somewhat obscure mountain plants, had a decidedly soporific effect on Paula. When the lights went up an hour and a half later, she found herself blinking owlishly, with the strong suspicion that she'd been at least half-asleep at least half of the time. Coffee and biscuits followed, and Paula gratefully accepted the reviving cup which Barry Lear brought her. He was ac-

companied by Andrés Peraza, a colleague from the
Institute where they both worked.

The two men seated themselves opposite her, looking
businesslike. Barry crossed his lean legs, and fixed her
with keen eyes.

'I've been thinking,' he announced. Relieved that he
was speaking English—his native Californian accent was
very pleasant, but his Spanish was frightful—Paula
nodded encouragingly.

'You know there's this debate coming up at the end
of the month—about Sa Virgen? Well, considering that
this is the first time someone from the Department of
the Environment ministry is coming, I feel we should
get Torres to attend, too. In person.'

'Nice idea,' she agreed. 'But as he's never come to any
of the other meetings, why should he come to this one?'

'Because you're going to ask him.'

'Me?'

'I have a feeling that you got through to Señor Torres.'
Barry manipulated his cup with sinewy fingers. 'He'll
listen to you. Maybe.'

'I don't know about that,' she said uncomfortably.

'It's worth a try, anyway. Don't you think?'

'What's worth a try?' she asked, trying not to sound
too suspicious.

'Your contacting him. And issuing an invitation in
person.'

'I already did that, on Sa Virgen——'

'No harm in doing it again.' Barry smiled thinly. 'He
might just come—if you ask him.'

'But why should he?'

'To see you again.' And before she could interrupt,
he went on, 'I've got a hunch about this, Paula. Maybe

you got on his nerves, or maybe you tickled his hormones, or maybe both.'

Andrés chuckled, but Paula didn't find it that funny. 'That's just guesswork,' she said.

'Sure. But I'm convinced you've stuck in his craw one way or another. If you were to ring him up, challenge him to be there—he might just do it.'

'Barry's got an instinct about these things.' Reinforcements had arrived in the form of a couple of the girls, both of them friends of Barry Lear's. The one who had spoken was called Julia Symmonds, and was English. 'I think it's a brilliant notion! If you could get Torres to that meeting, we'd make sure he'd have an evening he wouldn't forget in a hurry!'

Paula winced inside. While Barry Lear and his friends didn't belong to the lunatic contingent who'd invaded the island, screaming 'Hands off Sa Virgen' last year, they were definitely very committed to the environmental cause. Hardliners. Paula wasn't sure she liked the sound of Julia's promise.

'Don't worry,' Barry smiled, guessing her thoughts, 'no one's going to throw hand grenades. Any assault on Señor Torres is going to be strictly intellectual. We're scientists, remember, not hooligans.'

'It doesn't matter how sound our arguments are,' Julia put in, 'nobody's impressed by representatives, least of all the press. I mean, the government's sending a *representative*, and Torres is sending a *representative*—we'll be the only people appearing in person!'

'A collection of monkeys with no organ-grinder,' her friend nodded. 'It'd just be a sham.'

'But if Juan Torres was to be there in person—that would be news!'

'Exactly,' Barry confirmed. 'It would be a debate, rather than a lot of hot air. How about it?'

'Well...' To tell the absolute truth, Paula was far from keen to renew Juan Torres' acquaintance. But under the keen gaze of these determined conservationists, any vacillation was going to look like cowardice. Barry Lear was by way of being the doyen of the group. He was certainly one of the most highly qualified members, and he had the kind of presence which made him a natural, if rather ruthless, leader. She respected him deeply, and didn't want to seem uncommitted to the cause. 'Isn't it rather short notice—that's what he'll say, won't he?'

'He's got three full weeks to prepare. All he's going to be doing is answering questions, anyway.'

'I suppose so...but I don't know how to get in touch with him, anyway,' she finished lamely.

'We do,' Julia said with a short laugh.

Andrés nodded. 'Believe me, Paula, a lot of us have tried to speak to Torres.' He spoke English with a heavy Spanish accent. 'You never get past his secretaries and lawyers.'

'But maybe he'll speak to you,' Barry finished. 'And if you can get him to that meeting, you'll have done more to save Sa Virgen than any of us.'

'The press will be there for certain. If I can work my contacts with Majorca TV, which I'm sure I can, then so will the television cameras.' Julia's face was eager. 'The whole island will be watching. We'll out-argue him at every point. He'll end up looking such a villain that public opinion will swing right round to our side. It'll be a major step towards saving Sa Virgen.'

'You do want to save Sa Virgen, don't you?' asked one of the other girls pointedly. There were seven or eight people around her now, making her feel more than a little cornered.

'Of course I do,' she said. 'I love Sa Virgen!'

'Besides the fact that you love it,' Andrés said drily, 'it is also one of the few unspoiled Balearic islands left. Sa Virgen and Sa Dragonera are among the last refuges of the Eleonora's falcon. This is an important fight, Paula. More than your feelings are involved.'

'Paula's quite aware of the ecological importance of Sa Virgen,' Barry said to his colleagues sharply. 'Don't lecture her.'

'Sorry,' Andrés shrugged. 'I just feel very strongly. To you and Barry, this is maybe less emotional. But to me, a Majorcan—you understand?'

'Of course,' Paula nodded, but she was feeling extremely unhappy about all this. Why? Just because Torres made her shy? Or was it because the whole set-up was something like a betrayal?

'If you really care,' Julia pressed, 'this is something so easy to do...'

Paula gulped down her coffee, and nodded briskly. 'OK. I'll try, at any rate. What do you want me to do?'

'Attagirl.' Barry's voice was soft, but there was no mistaking his satisfaction. 'I'll give you his home number. It's not in the book. If you call him tomorrow at lunch time, he's certain to be there. OK?'

'OK,' she nodded, trying to look cheerful as Barry scribbled a number down on a notepad. The faces around her were excited, happy.

Barry passed her the number, and grinned. 'This could be our first real break. If it is, you're going to make a big difference to the fight for Sa Virgen, Saint Georgina.'

In the event, it was two days before she rang the number.

The reason for the delay was simple cowardice. Every time she'd picked up the phone to ring Juan Torres, her nerve had failed her. On Friday, though, she knew she had to have the courage of her convictions.

She called the number from work, feeling very nervous indeed, and was answered by what was clearly a male secretary or butler.

'I wonder if I could speak to Señor Torres, please?'

'I do not think that the *señor* is at home,' the voice replied flatly. 'Who is calling, please?'

'My name is Paula Castle,' she quavered.

'Would you care to leave a message?'

'Yes, please.' She didn't know whether she was relieved or disappointed at not speaking to Torres. Maybe a bit of both!

'One moment please, *señorita*.'

She made absent notes on the document she was translating while she waited. So much for Barry's idea that she would receive a rapturous welcome at the Torres household!

Then her pen froze over the paper as the deep voice suddenly entered her left ear.

'Paula Castle?'

'Oh—hello!' She had a sudden vision of that dark, crooked-nosed face, and it made her upper lip prickle with sweat. 'I thought you were out.'

'Not at home to callers,' he corrected drily. 'Which is not the same thing as "out". As a linguist, I'm sure you appreciate the difference.'

'Oh.' She remembered that husky tone all too well! 'All part of being a very private man, I suppose.'

He didn't rise to the bait. 'What can I do for you?'

She launched straight into it, keeping her voice bright and guileless. 'Oh, I just wanted to make sure you hadn't forgotten about the twenty-ninth.'

He paused. 'You'll have to enlighten me. It appears I have forgotten, after all.'

'The debate. About Sa Virgen.' She swallowed, her mouth feeling rather dry. 'It's being held in the Ramón Lull Hall, at seven-thirty on Friday the twenty-ninth. You said you'd be there.'

'I said I'd be represented,' he corrected her calmly.

'You're not coming?'

'I have no intention of doing so, no.'

'Oh.' This time, Paula injected scorn into her retort. 'I'd rather hoped you'd have the courage to show up for once.'

A chill drifted down the line. 'I don't need courage to face your rabble, Paula.'

'They're not a rabble! They're scientists and conservationists.'

'And which are you?'

'A conservationist.' She took a breath. 'But more than that, I'm someone who loves Sa Virgen, Señor Torres. And I'll never have the money to stay in one of your holiday chalets, not even for a week. So if you build that village, I'll be shut out of somewhere that means a great deal to me.'

His voice was bored. 'You wrench my heartstrings.'

'Urbanising Sa Virgen would be a shocking act of de-liberate vandalism!'

'But very profitable.' She could almost hear him yawn.

'How can you measure profit against the destruction of something so precious?' she demanded, so angry that she was twisting the telephone cord around her slim fingers.

'That's my prerogative. And, incidentally, my business. And now, if you have nothing else to say——'

'Wait!' she pleaded. 'You absolutely won't come to the meeting, then?'

'It's extremely unlikely,' he confirmed. Then, after letting the pause trickle on for a few seconds, he added, 'However...'

'However?' she prompted, snatching at the hint.

'However, I'm prepared to discuss it.'

'Fine.' Paula's hazel eyes were glowing now. 'Let's discuss it.'

'Not now. I have too much to do. Come and convince me over the weekend.'

Completely taken aback, Paula blinked. 'You want me to come to your house? To see you?'

'Yes.'

'What for?'

'If I were the woman, and you the man,' he said silkily, 'such reluctance would be considered ungallant.'

'But...' Her heart was beating so much faster that she was out of breath.

'Unless, of course,' he purred, '*you* are the one who lacks courage?'

'It's not that,' she lied. What on earth did he want to see her for? Phoning him had been bad enough. The thought of facing him again, on his own ground, was enough to make the hair prickle on her arms. Her thoughts flicked quickly to Barry and the group, and what they would say if she refused. 'If...if I come and see you, will you promise to attend that meeting?'

'No. The deal is that if you *don't* come and see me, I most certainly won't attend the meeting. On the other hand, if you can convince me to come...'

'I don't understand why you want to see me,' she stammered.

'You sound as though the prospect alarms you,' he drawled. 'What have you to fear from me?'

Paula thought of the dark, brooding strength in the man, and felt her skin prickle. 'N-nothing, I suppose.'

'Exactly. Nothing. So let's say Saturday afternoon at two-thirty.'

'I don't even know where you live!'

'Off the Esporles road, just before you get to the village of San Sebastian. You'll see a small sign to Alcamar. Take that road. *Hasta la vista*, Paula.'

Her own goodbye was rather stunned, and after she'd put the phone down, she stared at it as though it were a cobra that had just bitten her.

Maybe Barry Lear had been right. Maybe Torres, had, after all, been intrigued by her. Or was that insane vanity on her part? It really wasn't very likely that a man like Juan Torres could ever be very interested in someone as ordinary as herself. Far more likely that he had some ulterior motive. Something to do with Sa Virgen? It occurred to Paula with a flash of unease that both sides in this wrangle might be using her for their own ends.

Well, the only way to find out was to go and see. An electric arc of excitement jumped inside her, from heartbeat to heartbeat. An invitation to Juan Torres' house was probably the rarest commodity on the Majorcan social circuit. And she was very definitely *not* going to turn it down! Her mother would be boasting about this to her friends for months.

And this time, she vowed to herself, she was going to be prepared. Dressed right, looking right, feeling right. Let him see that there was a damn sight more to Paula Castle than a tousle-haired tomboy!

She scooped up her work, and made for the library with such an air of zeal that Señor Gomila, the senior partner, beamed approvingly from his office doorway.

On a thought, Paula stopped. "Señor Gomila, have you heard of Juan Torres?'

He surveyed her over his hornrimmed spectacles. 'You mean young Juan? Of course,' he nodded.

'Have you met him?'

'Many times. I knew his father well. Juan is very like him.' Inserting a wrinkled forefinger in the book he'd been studying, Jaime Gomila smiled absently into the past. 'His mother, now...ah, Paula, there was a beauty! Eyes like jet, a smile that could stop your heart from beating, hair like a cascade of black silk...' He shook his head reminiscently. 'She was stunning. She had all Majorca in a sweat over her.'

'Is she still alive?'

'No. No, she died a few years ago, with her husband.' Señor Gomila sighed, his lean shoulders dropping slightly. 'They were both killed in a tragic accident.'

'I'm sorry,' Paula said lamely, fully aware that her employer must have suffered a painful loss with the Torres' death. About to leave, she hesitated again. 'About Juan—the younger Juan, I mean—how did he break his nose?'

'In the same accident.' The lawyer nodded sadly. 'Yes, in the same accident. Such a pity about his face. He'd inherited his mother's good looks, you know.'

'He's still a supremely attractive man,' Paula smiled.

'Indeed?' Shrewd eyes twinkled at her. 'Is that what all these questions are about?'

'Oh, no. I'm not in Juan Torres' league! Still,' she mused, 'he could easily have that nose repaired. A good plastic surgeon would straighten it in no time.'

'Maybe he doesn't want it straightened.'

'Sorry?'

But Jaime Gomila merely smiled inscrutably over his book and retreated back into his office, leaving Paula to ponder on that last sentence.

Later in the afternoon, she called Barry to tell him about Juan Torres' invitation. The ornithologist was delighted. 'I told you he'd been stung, didn't I?' But he added, 'Make sure he comes to that meeting, Paula. Don't let him just waste your time.'

'I won't,' she promised, flushed with the excitement of the invitation. She was very glad, now, that she had agreed to do what he had asked! 'If it's possible to get him there, I'll do it.'

She worked an hour and a half late, which wasn't unusual, to be able to deliver the translated document to Jaime Gomila. As a consequence she was able to enjoy the drive home in her little Fiesta, with no rush-hour traffic to worry about.

The twilight made the old stones of Palma, always a lovely city, glow with a romantic golden light. Outside the city, the countryside was enchanted. Giant agaves lined the road, towering against the pink-stained sky, interspersed with yuccas, palms and prickly pears. Beyond the subtropical riot, fields of almond and fruit trees stretched out towards the violet hills.

As she rounded the bend, her face lit up with pleasure at the vista of stubby stone towers and high wooden sails among the orange groves. The windmills of

Majorca...such a lovely symbol of a kind of agri-
culture, a way of life, that was disappearing. Paula reflected for the thousandth time how lucky she was to
live in such a beautiful part of the world. If only people
were more aware of how fragile that beauty was! You
simply couldn't keep building and building and
building...sooner or later something had to give way.

Why couldn't Juan Torres see that? Was he just
blinded by greed? It was a problem puzzling enough to
bring a thoughtful frown to her normally smooth
forehead.

For someone so charming and obviously intelligent,
he seemed to have a weird blind spot. Unless he wasn't
nearly as charming and intelligent as she gave him credit
for. Which meant that *she*, and not he, was the blind
one. That fascinatingly crooked nose! In a way it
summed up the conflicting mixture she sensed in the man,
of brutality and strength allayed with kindness and
passion.

He was a difficult man to pin down. She'd called him
a natural enemy. Yet when you spoke to him, you felt
so alive, so *intense*... What would he be like as a friend?
Loyal, warm, authoritative.

As a lover?

That was a question which, though it made her squirm
uncomfortably in her seat, Paula had no possible way
of answering. Because the simple fact was that Paula
had never slept with a man in her life.

Being a virgin was something she felt both easy and
uncomfortable about. Easy because it was a completely
natural state. Uncomfortable because so few of her girlfriends seemed to share that state. Not by the age of
twenty-three, anyway. A twenty-three-year-old virgin? It
made you think there was something wrong somewhere.

A feeling that she must have shirked her duty in some way.

She'd always had plenty of boyfriends, and she had been tempted more than once to part with that mysterious commodity known as her maidenhood. What had always stopped her was the realisation that her motivation was suspect. It would be stupid to lose your virginity just for the sake of losing it. There had to be a better reason.

Like what? Like love, of course. A little smile crept across her mouth. *Love.* What the hell was love, anyway? What Mum felt for Dad? What Helen felt for her Spanish husband? Her parents appeared to share a kind of friendly tolerance. As for Helen and Diego, whatever went on between them, behind a locked door, it was always accompanied by plenty of giggling and squeaking, and had always inspired Paula with something less than reverence.

No, she didn't have much faith in the magic powers of sexual love. *Love* was what she felt for this wonderful landscape, for the unspoiled woods of Sa Virgen, for the feeling of *Sulky Susan* slicing through a blue sea. And whatever else might accompany the eventual loss of her maidenhood, she knew this—that it would only be an anticlimax!

Pondering on thoughts like these, she drove through the village, and into the yard with the three huge lemon trees. By the time she was locking the Fiesta, her thoughts had wandered back to a ruthless mouth, a pair of jet-black eyes, and a brutally crooked nose. It was pointless getting involved with the man on a personal level. She had to keep this businesslike.

For the first time, she was beginning to feel that there was some point to all of this. The campaign to save Sa

Virgen, which had already been going on for over six months, had been rather an amateur affair up till now, marked by the kind of horseplay and squabbling that alienated the public, rather than convinced them. So far, in fact, it had succeeded in precisely nothing except creating a little notoriety.

But getting Juan Torres to attend a serious debate, with an official from the Ministry of the Environment present as an observer, would be a serious step forward. It might make all the difference in capturing the heart of an indifferent public.

Well, she knew next to nothing about Juan Torres. Before she walked into his lair tomorrow, she'd better pump her mother for every scrap of information she could get!

CHAPTER THREE

IT RAINED all morning Saturday. Then, at lunch time, it stopped, leaving the air warm and humid, the sky patched here and there with bits of blue beyond the grey.

The ball of nerves in Paula's stomach had killed her appetite, and she hardly got a mouthful of lunch down, much to James' amusement.

'I told you the dark, dangerous type would be your downfall,' he grinned, helping himself to the lamb chop left on her plate. 'I've never seen you so love-sick.'

'I'm *not* love-sick,' she snapped. 'Just nervous about persuading him to come to the debate. I get the feeling he may just eat me this afternoon.'

Her father put in a snort. 'Does he have to supply his own tar and feathers?'

'It's going to be a discussion, not a lynching,' Paula said. 'We want him to put his own point of view.'

'So your tame wolves can tear him to pieces? Your sister's like Mowgli, the Jungle Boy,' he volunteered to James. 'She has this pack of savage beasts at her beck and call, called conservationists. Last year they occupied Sa Virgen en masse, and practically pulled the island down, stone by stone. One way, I suppose, of preventing any development.'

'You're not funny, Tom. Paula's friends had nothing to do with that, nor did Paula.' Dismissing her husband, Margaret turned back to Paula. 'What are you going to wear, dear? You look lovely in that blue dress with the white collar and cuffs.'

'Too young,' Paula decided.

'If he's going to eat you,' James offered unrepent-antly, 'how about just a light dressing of mustard? With some parsley on the salient bits, of course.'

'I love being taken seriously by everyone,' Paula said drily, getting up to go to her bedroom. 'Excuse me. The lamb has to prepare for the slaughter.'

The Esporles road was shiny with recent rain, and the countryside had a washed, clean look that in a few weeks would be giving way to the baked crispness of summer.

This was such a lovely time of year, the ravishing flush of almond blossom having given way to an abundance of green leaves and lush fields full of wildflowers. She was so intent on the beauty around her that she almost missed the sign to Alcamar, and had to reverse back along the road a hundred yards.

The turn-off road, which was well surfaced by Majorcan standards, climbed steadily for a few miles, the countryside becoming wilder and, to Paula's eyes, lovelier as it went on.

The great double-gates across the road were a surprise. Marble-columned, and ornamented with beautiful wrought iron, they brought her to a sudden halt, eyes widening. Beyond them stretched acres of oranges and lemons, and in the distance, a wooded hillside rose upwards.

As she hesitated, the gate swung a little way open, and a middle-aged man in peasant's clothes came out to meet her.

Paula wound down her window. '*Buenas tardes*. Is that Señor Juan Torres' property?'

He smiled. 'You have been on Don Juan's property since you left Esporles road. Are you Señorita Castle?'

'Yes.'

'Welcome. The master is expecting you. I will open the gate.'

The master? Typical serf mentality, she thought drily. This was like pre-revolutionary Russia, or some place where twentieth-century democracy hadn't yet arrived. Reflecting with some irony that she'd been driving on Juan Torres' private driveway for the past twenty minutes without knowing it, Paula drove through the opened gates, waved to the gate-keeper, and set off down the apparently endless avenue of immaculately tended citrus groves.

This man appeared to own half of the Mediterranean! If you squeezed all the oranges here, you'd have a lake of orange juice half a mile wide. It was almost shocking that one man should own so much land. It was hugely rich landowners like Juan Torres who shouldered the chief responsibility for the environment. And they were invariably the chief offenders.

She made a mental resolution that, come what may, she would give Torres a piece of her mind this afternoon. It was an opportunity too good to be missed! And, on a less pious note, it would at least be interesting to see how the really filthy rich lived.

There was at least another mile of oranges before she got to the house. She parked on the gravel drive, and got out to stare at it.

So this was what wealth and ruthlessness could achieve!

Made of stone the same colour as the surrounding hills, and softened by creeping ivy, Juan Torres' house stood massive and square on a little rise, overlooking the valley. The rows of tall, arched windows made it unusual among Majorcan houses, which tended to have fewer, and smaller windows. Some were shuttered, but those on the ground floors were all thrown open to the warm spring afternoon.

A high stone tower, obviously an ancient structure, dominated the rambling garden. It rose high above the roof of the main house, stark and dramatic.

An archway led into an inner courtyard, obviously the entrance to the house. In the absence of any welcoming-party, Paula walked through into the paved inner courtyard, noticing a carved stone plaque reading, '1634'.

The courtyard, equally deserted, was charming. Flowering trees in big pots had been arranged around a central fountain, which splashed peacefully in the silence. The high walls around made the place into a haven of tranquillity. Up one wall, an enormous bougainvillaea was already in pinky-purple bloom.

Parked inside was a vintage car, a red Ferrari, obviously very valuable. Trust Torres to drive something as conspicuous as that!

Paula stood in silence, dangling her bag in both hands, just drinking it in. No amount of hostility towards Juan Torres could blind her to the great beauty of the house. What a fabulous place this was! It had been loved and lived in for three and a half centuries. More than a house, it was a huge work of art created by time and generations of human effort.

She turned quickly as she heard the footsteps behind her. A flight of marble steps curved down from a doorway within the courtyard, and the man she had come to see was walking down towards her.

He was wearing the same sort of fine-quality grey jersey he'd worn on Sa Virgen, simple and stylish; however, the denims and boots had been replaced by charcoal trousers and beautiful hand-made shoes. She'd remembered Torres' height, and his commanding presence. But she'd forgotten the brooding sensuality in his eyes and mouth, the impact of that broken nose. He stopped in front of her, the intensity in his dark eyes doing odd things to her heart.

God, he was handsome! That tanned, sculpted face, with its disturbing mark of violence, was actually beautiful. His eyes were black pools into which a woman's soul could sink and drown...

'Well,' she said brightly, breaking the silence with false jollity, 'here I am.'

'Here you are,' he agreed quietly. He reached out and lifted the sunglasses off her face, as if to be sure he hadn't forgotten what she looked like. Feeling oddly naked, she tried to return his dark stare, but felt her mouth quiver with nerves.

'Here you are, indeed. But rather different from the last time I saw you.'

Was that all? It had taken her over an hour and a half to get ready for this meeting!

It had been the memory of Cristina Colom's elegance that had finally decided Paula to go for sophistication. She'd painstakingly braided the mass of her chestnut hair, and wound it into a chignon that coiled like a thick, glossy viper around her head, leaving the slender beauty of her neck and jawline free. Her make-up was minimal, just enough to gloss her full mouth and point up the soft hazel of her eyes.

The tailored suit she wore, soft peach-coloured linen belted at the waist, was the most elegant thing she had. On her feet she wore neat, pretty tan court shoes that matched her belt and bag.

She'd never looked more lovely or desirable in her life, and Paula had enough intelligence to know that. So she couldn't help the flash of disappointment that darkened her eyes momentarily at Juan Torres' apparent indifference.

It was just a flicker, but Juan Torres didn't miss it. Laughing softly, he leaned forward, and with disbelief she felt warm lips plant a brief kiss on her own mouth, before she had time to quickly draw back. 'It's an improvement on jeans,' he informed her gravely. 'Welcome to Alcamar. Come.'

Feeling as though she were floating on air, she let him guide her into the great house. The room she found herself in was cool and high-ceilinged, and very large. It was beautifully furnished as a sitting-room, with Persian rugs on the floor, some wonderful Majorcan antiques, and fine wood panelling on the walls.

A maid was just setting out coffee from a silver tray—the gate-keeper must have rung ahead of her arrival—and a huge vaseful of early roses on an antique table was perfuming the air. In one corner of the room, a magnificent oak staircase rose upwards to the floor above.

It was very, very hard not to be overawed by all this wealth and taste. She'd been in sumptuous houses before, but this place was different. It had an atmosphere that was as unique as the man who owned it, a quality that made you feel very small. She could still feel that kiss on her lips, warm and masculine. Had it been meant as an insult, or something more like a...challenge?

She accepted the coffee he poured her, and settled herself into a sofa.

'You must forgive my ignorance, Señor Torres,' she said formally, 'but until today I'd never heard of Alcamar, though I must have driven past the sign a hundred times. What does the name mean?'

He nodded at the ruined tower, visible through one of the arched windows. 'That is Alcamar. Or what remains of Alcamar. It was a fortress built by the Arabs, when they ruled the Western Mediterranean a thousand years ago. They called it El Quamar, which means the Tower of the Moon. There's a view of the whole valley from the ramparts. Later on, I will take you to the top.'

His tone made that a command, rather than an invitation. 'An Arab tower,' she said. 'Does that mean you have Moorish ancestry?'

'Probably.' The glittering black eyes underlined the probability. It was somehow easy to imagine him in another age, wearing a burnous, and slitting infidel throats. She felt a sudden awareness of being very much in the lion's den.

'You have a lot of orange trees,' she commented.

'Around a quarter of a million,' he said calmly.

Her eyes opened wide. 'That many? My God—that's a tree for every man, woman and child in Palma!'

'You make it sound like a crime to own orange trees,' he said, picking up her disapproving tone.

'I don't think it's a crime, no,' she answered coolly. 'Owning land is not morally wrong in itself.'

'I'm glad to hear it,' he said, with just a hint of satire.

'The morality comes into how that land is treated,' she continued, meeting his eyes. 'Whether it's exploited and destroyed. Or whether it's left unspoiled for future generations.'

'Thank you for the lesson,' he said with a slight bow. 'I must remember to jot that down in my diary.'

Returning sarcasm for sarcasm, Paula smiled thinly. 'To tell the truth, señor, I'm pleasantly surprised to find that you're not one of the idle rich, as I had imagined.'

'There is nothing idle about being an *estanciero*,' he retorted, with a glitter in his dark eyes. 'I planted half those trees myself. And by that, I mean with my own hands.' She glanced involuntarily at his hands, resting on his hips. Beautiful hands, but full of power, too. Strong man's hands, made to work and fight, as well as to caress the smooth flanks of a woman.

'Oh, I believe you about the orange trees,' she said, sipping her coffee elegantly. 'You needn't labour the point—it's all most impressive. And now that I see you're actually a man of the soil, rather than a pampered playboy, I feel sure that you'll appreciate the points I want to make this afternoon.'

That her barb had lodged was evident by the way he stiffened.

'I have worked on Alcamar winter and summer, since I was a boy of twelve,' he said coldly. 'Since before you were born to sail your yacht and show discourtesy to strangers. I assure you, I have often wished with all my heart to be one of the idle rich, as you call them— Alcamar is a hard mistress.' His smile was ironic. 'Such was not my destiny, however.'

'You wrench my heartstrings,' she said with daring impudence, echoing his own words. 'Alcamar may be a hard mistress,' she pressed on quickly, 'but also a very beautiful one. You can hardly expect me to feel sorry for you—being the master of all this.'

'No. I do not ask for your pity.' He'd been standing, but now he came to sit beside her, resting his right ankle on his left knee. 'But we are not here to discuss Alcamar.'

'No,' she agreed briskly, 'we're not.' Putting down her empty cup, she picked up her bag, and took out the sheaf of printed stuff inside. 'I've brought you some reading matter, Señor Torres.'

'How charming,' he said, his cutting tone meaning exactly the reverse. 'Some more coffee?'

'Thank you, no.' She waited until he'd poured himself a second cup, then went on. 'There are several documents you ought to read in this file,' she informed him in a schoolmarmish way. 'Maybe even *you* can learn something you didn't know. This, for example, is a leaflet about Sa Virgen which was printed by the Environmental Group last year.'

'Ah, yes.' Juan's dark, thick brows had lowered ominously as she held out the document, most of which had been compiled by Barry Lear. 'I've read this masterpiece.' He picked the green and yellow thing out of her hand, as though handling some poisonous reptile. 'It's a farrago of lies and hysteria.'

'Oh?' Paula pulled her dress straight in a manner that suggested she was preparing for battle. 'Point out the lies in it.'

'It's one long lie,' he shrugged, flicking it open. 'The insinuation that I'm about to destroy the natural habitat of Sa Virgen is pure invention. This so-called scientist talks of my covering the island with concrete apartments.'

'He's not a so-called scientist,' she said indignantly, stung by his tone. 'He's a friend of mine, and he happens to be a highly respected authority on birdlife!'

'I know what he is,' Juan said contemptuously. 'Barry Lear is a guest on this island, but he lacks a guest's manners. He is a fanatic and a troublemaker. You call him a friend of yours?'

'I admire his commitment,' she said stiffly, meeting the dark eyes. 'No doubt he seems like a fanatic to you, because he stands in the way of your raking in another few millions. But people like him care very much about the environment, and they're the only ones on this island who are doing something about it!'

'You speak like an infatuated schoolgirl,' he said coolly.

'Oh?' she said, keeping her temper with an effort. 'I'm sorry to disappoint you, then.'

'Don't confuse neurotic aggression with dedication, Paula. They are not the same thing at all.'

'I wouldn't expect someone like you to have a balanced opinion of a man like Barry Lear,' she flashed back. 'So you can spare me the propaganda against him!'

'Propaganda?' He lifted a disdainful eyebrow. 'Your friend Lear is the one who specialises in propaganda. His accusations are absurd. Even you must see that they are lies. I intend to build a very small group of chalets on a single site near Cala Lom, not a vast concrete city. There will be no more building after that, and certainly no motorised transport allowed.'

'Except helicopters,' Paula reminded him sharply. 'Though I forgot—the falcons actually *like* the noise of helicopters, don't they?'

'Don't be an idiot. I never said that. What I *did* say was that one helicopter flight a week will not disturb the falcons.'

'That's hard to believe,' she snorted.

He ran lean fingers impatiently through his thick, slightly curly hair. 'Your mental image of helicopters obviously comes from violent films on television. What do you imagine?' he demanded with scorn. 'Some olive-green monster roaring in the sky, spitting bullets and rockets at the wildlife? The modern transport helicopter is quiet, quick and efficient. It doesn't pollute the air or the water. And it avoids the currents which can, as you very well know, be fierce.'

'You're so sure of yourself,' she said, trying not to look overawed by the force of his response. 'How on earth can you assess the impact that all this technology is going to have on Sa Virgen? The truth is, you can't! For millions of years the island's been at peace. Now it's going to be exposed to noise, machinery, and above all, people. It's the beginning of the end, can't you see that?' Her lip curled. 'Or has the prospect of all those extra *pesetas* blinded you to every social responsibility?'

He stared at her through ominously narrowed eyes, and for a moment she quailed inwardly. 'Well,' she said defensively, 'you shouldn't have asked me to come here today if you didn't want to hear any opposition. I take it you had some purpose in wanting me here?'

'Yes,' he said brusquely, 'I did have a purpose. Perhaps it's best if we come to it now, and stop wasting time.' He finished his coffee, then rose. 'Come,' he commanded, crooking a finger at her. 'I want to show you something.'

He led her to a polished oak staircase, and she climbed the creaking steps to the room above, wondering.

This room was clearly a library. Built on the same grand scale as the sitting-room below, it was entirely lined with shelves upon shelves of books, their richly colored leather spines gleaming with gold leaf in the soft light.

The centre of the room was taken up by a huge reading-table, upon which was a detailed scale model of an island.

'Sa Virgen!'

'Yes. Sa Virgen.' He watched her as she approached the model, eyes widening as she took in the size and detail of the model.

'It's exquisite. It must have taken someone ages to build this!' The top of Puig Virgen was higher than her own head, and the landscape had been rendered with meticulous detail. 'Here's Cala Vibora, and there's the beach...' She traced her route into the little bay with her forefinger.

'And this is the cliff where we met,' he pointed out. 'It's the other side, though, that I want you to see.' He took her round the massive table to the northern side of the island. Nestling above the sweep of Cala Lom was a small group of structures. Paula had to stoop to see the details of tiled roofs, blue pools, and the flat circle of a landing-pad for helicopters. Against the scale of the island, the projected village was tiny. And not unattractive.

'The impact on Sa Virgen,' he said forcefully, 'is going to be negligible. The ground is flat and bare there, so no trees will have to be felled. You can see how far it is from the nesting sites, and that it's virtually impossible to get to Cala Vibora from the village.' He tapped the miniature landing-pad with lean fingers. 'You can also see that the helicopters will never overfly the island. They'll come straight across the sea from Palma and land right there. There will be far less noise than that made by commercial airliners and military jets every day.'

In silence, she looked at the beautiful model. Viewed like this, it was hard to sustain her feelings of righteous indignation.

'Over here,' he went on briskly, moving to a smaller table by a window, 'is a model of one of the chalets. Even someone as prejudiced as you would agree that it's not a particularly ugly design.'

Paula studied that, too, in silence. It was, in fact, a beautiful design, with enough traditional Majorcan elements to make it blend in perfectly with the rugged landscape of Sa Virgen.

'As developments go,' she said slowly at last, 'I have to admit that this is one of the better ones I've seen.' She shot him a quick glance. 'If these models are accurate, that is.'

'They are.'

'But there's a feature you can't plan in advance, and that happens to be the most important feature of all. The people. It would take only one of them to start a forest fire in summer, and there would be an ecological disaster.'

'We had a bad fire on Sa Virgen ten years ago,' he said drily. 'It was started by a pair of naturists camping out there without permission. Every year or two there's a blaze started up by some environment-loving trespasser.' He met her eyes with a hard glance. 'People not unlike you, Paula.'

'That's a cheap shot!'

'But an accurate one. People with comfortable kitchens in their own chalets, on the other hand, don't need to light fires in the woods.' He nodded at the scale model. 'There'll be a permanent staff at the village, in any case, including an expert guide and a maintenance crew, equipped to deal with any emergency, human or natural.'

'You can't police your guests all of the time. You'd never be sure that some of them weren't misbehaving somewhere in the island!'

'That applies to any kind of hotel, anywhere. But Sa Virgen is hardly going to attract destructive people.'

'Oh?' she quirked an eyebrow. 'Are the rich morally better than the poor?'

'No. But Sa Virgen will be marketed as a holiday specifically for people who want peace, solitude, and a natural setting. There will be no shops, no fairgrounds, no nightclubs, no discotheques.'

'But can't you see . . .' Paula launched straight into the counterattack, and he listened impatiently to her arguments. As she wrangled with Juan Torres, the sun was coming out, and starting to stream down through the windows, filling the room with a warm golden light. Out over the island they were discussing, falcons would be soaring in the washed air . . .

For almost an hour she kept up her attack, quoting every possible objection that could be raised. But Juan had an answer to everything. For the first time, she was beginning to realise how carefully thought out and meticulously planned the Sa Virgen project was. Very far from being a crude attempt to ruthlessly exploit the island's beauty, it was a very subtle and intelligent project. And she was beginning to realise just how ill-equipped she herself was to meet a man of Juan Torres' calibre in a head-on argument. It would require a much sharper and better informed mind—like Barry Lear's—to match up to this man.

'So much of this is news to me,' she said at last, studying the model with thoughtful eyes. 'I've never seen any of this before.'

'Naturally not. Nobody has. These details are confidential. I've been planning them for a long, long time.' His eyes narrowed significantly. 'And I'm *not* keen on the idea of being obstructed.'

She didn't miss the menace in his tone. 'OK. But even if your plan is better than most people imagine, that only bears out my point—that it would have been much better if you'd made everything public a long time ago. You haven't helped your own case by refusing to discuss the details with concerned bodies.'

'There has never been the slightest legal obligation on me to discuss my plans with anyone,' he retorted.

'But a lot of people think there's a moral obligation,' she pointed out. 'You could reassure them by telling them the truth.'

'Don't tell me,' he smiled ironically, 'that you're starting to approve of my scheme?'

'Not exactly,' she admitted carefully. 'I'd rather that not a single drop of cement was mixed on Sa Virgen. But I agree that this is at least a partial solution to the problem of building a holiday centre in an ecologically vulnerable zone. And I *do* think that you should come to that meeting at the twenty-ninth, and give people a better idea of what you intend to do.'

'Do you think people—the sort of people who'll be at that meeting—are capable of appreciating any of this?' he asked with patent disbelief written on his face.

'Well, I know that you can't take this model to the Ramón Lull Hall. But you should go, all the same. It's important that you answer your critics for once—in person, and not through representatives.'

He met her eyes directly. 'Not even if one of those representatives is you?'

Light dawned on her. 'So *that's* your little scheme,' she snapped. 'Make a useful convert out of one of the enemy! You thought you could win me over today, and get me to put in a good word for you on the twenty-ninth?'

'That's putting it a little crudely,' he drawled. 'But in essence—yes, I had hoped you would change your mind this afternoon, and in turn help others to change their minds.'

'Not on your life,' she retorted briskly. 'My mind hasn't been changed that much, I assure you. I'm still firmly on the side of the falcons, Señor Torres.'

'Then you still oppose the project?'

'I certainly don't support it,' she told him firmly. 'And as for propagandising Proyecto Virgen, you can do your own dirty work!'

They stared at one another in a taut silence for a long moment. Then he tossed down the pen he had been holding, with an expression that was not totally unsatisfied. "*Bueno*. At least you have seen the truth. That's a start. And that's enough about Sa Virgen for the time being. Let's not waste the whole afternoon arguing. You must see something of Alcamar.'

Again, that distinct impression that it was an order, not a suggestion! She suppressed a sigh as she nodded agreement. She'd done her best. At least the man was showing *some* regard for the concern about Sa Virgen. It was up to him to decide whether to attend the meeting, and any further pressing on her part would be counterproductive.

'I'd love to see the Goyas,' she said, remembering something her mother had told her last night.

He turned to her with a quick frown. 'The Goyas? What makes you ask that?'

'Rumor has it your family owns two fabulous paintings by Goya,' she smiled. 'Or is that just another myth in the Torres mystique?'

'Ah.' His expression eased. 'I regret that you can't see the Goyas right now. But if you're interested in paintings, I can show you two other canvases of some merit.'

'Yes, please!'

'Come, then.' He escorted her down the library, and through the door at the other end.

This section of the house, dim and cool because of the shuttered windows, had a mysterious quality; virtually every piece of furniture was an antique, and there was hardly a thing to be seen that bore the stamp of the twentieth century. As he led her through room after room, Paula had the overwhelming impression of the time that had passed here—of the centuries that had accumulated, the people who had lived and loved here.

'This house is like something that's been distilled over hundreds of years,' she said at last, as they entered the final room in the wing.

He looked at her quizzically. 'What do you mean?'

'Oh...' Paula struggled for words to express herself. 'It's as though everyone who's lived in this house has added something, some precious thing—a piece of furniture, or a painting, or maybe just a ghost.' She shivered slightly. 'Something that's been left behind them to say "I lived here, too". It gives the house a very rich, deep feeling... oh, it's useless trying to explain,' she finished on a little laugh. 'I don't really know what I mean myself.'

'I know what you mean,' he said quietly. 'You don't have to explain, Paula.'

He threw the shutters open, flooding the room with light. At the far end, two large oil paintings hung on either side of an inlaid English credenza. As Paula approached, she saw that they were full-length portraits of a young man and woman. Judging by the clothes they wore, they had been painted some thirty years ago.

'They're beautiful,' she said, and she meant both the paintings and their subjects. They were indeed strikingly handsome people. She knew instinctively who they were; even if Jaime Gomila hadn't already told her about the hair like black silk, and the eyes like jet, she'd have known the woman as Juan's mother. Her striking colouring was exactly like his; and the man, proud and handsome, had the same imposing stature and fine figure as his son.

Paula stared at the paintings in silence for a long time. 'Who painted them?' she asked at last.

'Salvador Dali,' he answered. 'Besides being the doyen of the surrealists, he was also a very fine portrait painter.'

'They're exceptional works,' Paula said quietly. 'They must be worth a fortune.'

'They won't be sold while I'm alive,' he said shortly.

'When did your parents die?' she asked hesitantly, not sure whether she was trespassing.

'Ten years ago.'

'How old were you then?'

Juan's eyes glinted. 'Twenty... something.'

Paula had to laugh. Why so coy?'

'I'm not telling you my age.'

'Why ever not?'

'I don't want you thinking of me as decrepit.'

She couldn't stop her eyes from dropping to his lean, muscular body. 'I'm hardly likely to think that,' she said softly, then coloured, and looked back at the portrait of his father. 'I'm twenty-three. I suppose that seems absurdly young to you.'

'It seems young,' he agreed gently. 'But not absurdly so. You are a mature, beautiful woman at twenty-three. If you must know, I'm thirty-six. I suppose that seems very old to you?'

'You've got one foot in the grave,' she smiled, then shot him a brief glance from under long eyelashes. 'I'd guessed you were thirty-six. In fact, I guessed your age the first moment I saw you.'

'Clever Paula,' he said softly.

There was something so intimate about the moment, such a contrast to the relentless fencing they'd been engaged in all afternoon, that Paula felt the goose-flesh spreading across her skin, nerves tightening in her stomach. She kept her eyes steadfastly fixed on the painting before her, not wanting him to guess at any of the disturbing thoughts going through her woman's mind. 'Your father was a very handsome man. He must have been about the same age as you are now when this portrait was painted.'

'Yes,' he nodded, 'more or less.'

The two pairs of dark eyes smiled down at them from the canvas, giving Paula courage to ask her next question. But before she could frame the words, Juan went on, 'You want to know how it happened?'

'I was wondering, yes. But if you don't want to...'

'It was a motor accident,' he explained briefly. 'The car was forced off the road by a tourist bus, on the way to Cabo Formentor. It fell down the cliff to the rocks below.'

Paula could only stare at him. She knew the road well enough to visualise the horror of the scene all too clearly. 'I'll never go on that road again,' she said quietly at last. 'I think I've always hated it.' Unconsciously, she touched his arm. 'I'm so sorry, Juan. I don't know what else I can say. I know you were in the car when it happened.'

'I don't usually like to speak of it.' He shrugged. 'But with...some people...it seems easier.' He was looking into her eyes as he spoke, and Paula felt that wave of weakness wash over her again, taking her breath away. This man who was supposed to be her enemy was starting to exert an uncanny power over her feelings.

But, as though unwilling to let the emotion of the moment develop any further, he turned and walked to

the window. 'Let's go out into the garden,' he commanded, closing the shutters, and darkening the room
once more. 'It's blasphemy not to enjoy that sunshine.'

As they went to the door in the soft darkness, she
bumped against him accidentally. It was the lightest of
touches, his hard side brushing her arm and the soft swell
of her breast for a second. He had touched her before,
on Sa Virgen. But this contact seemed to scorch her sensitive skin, and she felt it burning for long minutes afterwards. Nor did he speak to her again until they had
reached the sunlit garden outside.

When at last he turned to her to point out some feature
of the garden, there was something subtly warmer about
Juan Torres' expression. It matched her own feeling, that
over the past few hours they had changed from enemies
into something much closer and more complex.

He led her down one of the paved paths that led
through the big, rather riotous grounds. At the end of
it, past an old brick wall, was a sunken, rectangular
garden that had obviously been laid out in Arab times.
With a mossy fountain as its centrepiece, it was framed
by walkways that were arched over with trellises of roses.

'How lovely!' she exclaimed as she came through the
arched entrance. Bruised by the recent rain, the big pink
and white flowers were deliciously perfumed, and bees
were at work among the moist petals.

It enchanted Paula so much that she wandered along
the paved cloister in a dream, not minding the occasional cool drip that fell from the flowers above.

She did, however, gasp with shock when a very defi-
nite squirt of cold water invaded her happy trance. And
when she stepped aside, yet another jet sprayed her cheek
thoroughly, making her yelp in surprise and alarm.

Juan's strong hands guided her out of the danger zone. 'It pays to keep your eyes open at Alcamar,' he said gravely.

Now that she looked carefully, the whole cloister ahead was criss-crossed by decorative jets of water, making a silvery, almost imperceptible lattice-work to trap the unwary wanderer.

'Our Arab predecessors had a robust sense of humour,' he pointed out.

'You might have warned me,' she said in disgust, taking out a hanky to mop her neck.

'You were obviously thinking so hard about eco-logical matters that it seemed a shame to interrupt,' he smiled. 'Besides, these cloisters get a new victim all too seldom. It seemed a shame to spoil a thousand-year-old joke. Here, let me do that.'

He took the hanky from her, and started drying the water from her face and neck.

Standing so near to him, with those dark eyes intent on what he was doing, was not exactly soothing. His closeness, and the gentle touch of his fingers, brought the blood remorselessly to her face, and there was nothing she could do about it, but stand in a schoolgirl silence as the flush spread rosily across the skin of her throat, and up into her cheeks.

If he noticed her warm condition, he made no ac-knowledgement of the fact. As he leaned forward to mop the last droplets from her fine skin, Paula caught the warm, male smell of him, undercut by some expensive, non-sweet aftershave that was very attractive.

'My apologies,' he said, giving her back her hanky with a wicked expression in his eyes that was definitely not apologetic. 'May I ask what perfume you are wearing?'

'None,' she said in surprise. 'I never wear perfume.'

'You don't need to,' he said, eyes studying her mouth. 'Your skin smells like rose-petals without any need of perfume.'

'That's silly,' she looked up at him with nervous hazel eyes. 'You're smelling the real roses up above us.'

'Am I?' He bent forward, his lips almost touching the side of her neck, just under her ear, as if to inhale the smell of her soft skin. And this time, Paula felt her body sway towards Juan, so close that her breasts brushed against him. Her eyes were closed, all her senses fixed on the warm lips that had come so close to caressing her skin. If he had taken her in his arms there and then, and kissed her mouth, she would have responded to him not as a stranger, but as the most overwhelming man she had ever known.

But he simply drew back and smiled down at her mockingly. 'No,' he said, shaking his head, 'it's pure Paula. Perhaps more like honeysuckle than roses, but your skin definitely smells sweet. But the tower awaits. There is a way through the water—come, I'll show you.'

Paula let him lead her through the garden to the tower. If he was hoping to demolish her confidence with sheer male charm, she thought bemusedly, he was doing a damned good job of it. She was no match for him at this kind of game, either.

The tower's high, massive bulk commanded the whole property. There was a studded oak door at the foot of the tower, and as he pushed it open, Juan turned to her.

'This calls for good legs. How fit are you?'

'Fit as a flea,' she assured him confidently.

'No stopping, then,' he ordered, and hustled her up the stairs.

CHAPTER FOUR

THE stone staircase inside was broad enough, but it curved in a tight, steep spiral upwards. It was also dark, and much harder going than Paula had imagined. By the time they reached the first landing, Paula was out of breath, and by the second landing, her legs were on fire.

'You're going too fast,' she gasped. 'I have to rest——'

'At the top.' Relentlessly, he dragged her upwards, and she had to scurry along at his pace, cursing him, her own self-confidence and the Arab architects of the tenth century! Just when she was absolutely frantic for breath, and about to collapse on the cool stones, light glimmered down from above to give her strength for the last, painful burst.

'God,' she panted, sagging against the wall at the top, 'I'm—practically—dead!'

'After that little climb?' he scorned. He wasn't even breathing hard, and she gave him a black look between gasps.

'You do this—three or four—times a day—I suppose?'

'Not exactly. But perhaps I'm used to it.'

'I suppose your friend Cristina Colom just sails up?' Paula enquired drily. Cristina had been in her thoughts a lot today, but this was the first time she'd mentioned her name.

'Cristina takes it at a more sedate pace,' he smiled.

Damn! What had given her the childish hope that
Cristina hadn't been here with him? 'So why did I have
to be rushed up it, then?'

'You said you were so fit.'

'Not as fit as I thought I was. Phew, I'm hot!' The
upward charge had shaken her chignon partly loose, and
she struggled to set things right with both hands. 'Curse
this hair!' she muttered. 'I swear I'm going to have it
cut off next week.'

'Don't even think of it,' he said, so sharply that she
paused, her elbows on either side of her face, and looked
at him.

'Why not?'

'Why not?' he echoed. 'You who accuse *me* of vandalism ought to know why not. Your hair is an area of
outstanding natural beauty, and I hereby make an in-
junction against your ever cutting it.'

'You sound like my father,' she complained. But she
was inwardly delighted by the backhanded compliment.
To hear another remark like that, she'd gladly have run
down *and* back up again! 'Anyway,' she concluded, 'it'd
be a lot more manageable if you didn't make me shake
it loose.'

'Stop complaining,' he commanded, 'and come to see
the view.'

She obeyed. Despite all her carping, the violent exercise had exhilarated her, and the blood was pulsing
through her veins. And the view from the battlements
was absolutely stunning.

'What a sight,' she gasped. Clinging to the stones with
cautious hands, she looked down. 'Gosh! I hadn't realised how high up we are. You can see half the island
from here.'

'You can see Palma, at any rate—and sometimes as far as Ibiza.' He pointed out the cathedral, and the golden sweep of beach at Arenal, to the east. The Torres land stretched out for several kilometres all round, acres upon acres of citrus groves. She could see the distant grey ribbon of the Esporles road winding along the boundary. Behind them, the tiled roof of the villa gleamed in the sun, and above, the mountains slept all around.

'Did you really plant over a hundred thousand trees with your own hands?' she asked in awe, looking at the fertile, rich landscape all around them.

'Yes. To tell the absolute truth, three or four of my men helped me.' He paused. 'It might have been better if I hadn't turned a spade of earth.'

'Why do you say that?' she asked, turning to him. 'You've made this valley bloom. The smell of the orange blossom in summer must be fantastic!'

'We call it the *azahar*,' he nodded. 'Yes, the smell of the orange blossom in summer makes up for many things.'

'It's hard to believe.' Actually seeing the acres of dark green leaves, it was incredible to think of the work that had gone into Alcamar. 'How long does it take to plant a hundred thousand trees?'

'Ten years.'

'Ten years!'

'Measured by Alcamar's time, that is just a moment,' he said, as though he found her reaction naïve.

'I suppose,' she went on, trying to sound relaxed, 'this place explains your family name, too? *Torres* means "tower".'

'Exactly,' he nodded. 'Just as you are called Castle because your family once lived in one.'

'In the shadow of one, more likely.' She glanced at him. 'My brother believes there's no chance of compromise between us, because of our names alone.'

'A castle and a tower,' he said pensively. 'That is undoubtedly a warlike combination. We shall have to see, shall we not?'

His eyes challenged her again, and she tried to look insouciant. 'Quite.'

'Who knows,' he said softly, 'the coincidence may even mean that there is an inherent affinity between us?'

'Not about Sa Virgen,' Paula retorted briskly, determined not to quite forget why she was here.

'No,' he agreed, amused, 'not about Sa Virgen.'

She sighed over the view. 'If I'd done what you've done, and all this belonged to me,' she mused, 'I'd come up here every day for an hour, just to look at the view I'd created.'

'I used to do just that when I was a boy,' he nodded. 'Though it was strictly forbidden in those days, because the tower was crumbling, and very dangerous. I restored it a few years ago.'

She turned to lean back against the weathered old stones, and studied him. He was staring out over his land, Paula thought, like a brooding eagle.

'Have you lived here on your own since your parents died?' she asked.

He spoke slowly, as though his mind were on other things. 'More or less. My sister Isabella lived with me until three years ago, when she got married.'

'Is she older than you?'

'Younger, by a year. She lives just outside Madrid, with her husband. They have two children. But to answer your question—yes, apart from the staff, I live alone at Alcamar.'

'"Alone"?' she echoed. 'Not "lonely"?'

'Why should I be lonely?'

'Without a family, I mean.'

He glanced at her for the first time, his expression disdainful. 'I suppose you think I should marry, and fill this garden with screaming children?'

'That might be nice,' Paula ventured. 'Other people do it all the time.'

'Odd,' he snorted, 'how no woman can bear to think of a man surviving his thirtieth year unmarried. It can be done, you know.'

'You don't miss female company?'

'I can assure you, Paula, that I have a good deal more female company than I would if I were married,' he said with a dry note in his deep voice.

'Oh.' Paula didn't disguise her disapproving expression. 'I see.'

'You can take that prurient look off your face right now,' he said, aiming a lean forefinger at her. 'I'm not promiscuous. All I meant was that I enjoy the company of women—and I have a number of female friends, who would certainly not be tolerated by a wife.'

'Not by a jealous, insecure wife,' she acknowledged. 'But a sensible wife would never try and keep you from your friends. And this place...' She looked away from him at the rambling garden, and thought of the shuttered, unused rooms in the villa. 'Well, it needs a woman's touch.'

'You must draw your philosophy from frivolous magazines,' he scoffed.

'Marriage and children are very far from frivolous subjects,' she said, responding to his contempt with a flush.

He watched her for a moment, as though assessing her sincerity. 'Very well,' he said gravely. 'Assuming you're right—who do you suggest?'

'Oh . . . you know better than I do.' She glanced at him quickly with big hazel eyes. 'What about Señorita Colom?'

'A distinct possibility,' he nodded, without changing his expression. 'She has beauty, a very large fortune indeed—and she shares your opinion that Alcamar needs a woman's touch.'

Paula digested that painful morsel in silence. So Cristina was eager to marry Juan Torres. Well, why not? Any spinster would be. Juan was probably the target of many a scheming *mam*. 'And are you going to marry Cristina?' she asked at last.

'Perhaps,' he said casually, sounding almost bored.

'She's very beautiful,' Paula said in a dead voice. That little word *perhaps* had clouded the sky and cooled the sun for her, and she shivered, rubbing the sudden goose-flesh on her arms. 'She was very angry with me that day on Sa Virgen.'

'I can't think why,' he said formally, 'when you were being so charming.'

Paula couldn't suppress her snort of laughter. 'Well, now that you know exactly how fanatical I am, will you still let me trespass on Sa Virgen?'

'Any time you want.' His smile put the sun back into the afternoon. 'Though I mean what I said about your hair. Cut off so much as an inch, and you'll never set foot on Sa Virgen again.'

'Ever?'

'Ever.'

'At the rate it grows,' she wailed, 'it'll be down to my waist in a couple of years.'

'It's beautiful,' he said firmly. 'I love to see a woman's hair loose—though I have to admit that pigtail affair is . . . acceptable.'

'This "pigtail affair",' she rebuked him acidly, 'took me nearly an hour to do. I'm so glad you find it *acceptable*.'

'Well, it's coming loose again.'

'Damn . . .' She lifted her hands to rearrange it. Why did something always happen to spoil her poise?

'Let me try.' She dropped her arms, and stood obediently still as he moved behind her.

She felt his fingers tugging the pins loose, letting the heavy plait fall down her neck.

'It's as thick as my wrist,' he marvelled softly. 'And so glossy! It's like you—beautiful, healthy and young.' His touch was gentle, firm, almost like a caress. Her heart had skipped a beat at the unexpected tenderness of that deep voice, so close to her ear, and now it was beating faster, forcing Paula to breathe quicker.

He turned her to face him, and she found herself looking up, mesmerised, into Juan's dark eyes. The force of his personality was overwhelming, seeming to flood her senses. He lifted his hand to caress her face.

'Tell me,' he murmured, 'is your interest in me confined to Sa Virgen?'

'I—I don't understand,' she stammered.

'I think you do.' His fingers were trailing down her sides, spreading to cup each flank of her slim waist. 'You're so taut. So graceful. When I first saw you on Sa Virgen, you were like some wild thing that belonged on the island. I had the strangest feeling . . .'

'What?' she whispered as he tailed off on a smile.

'That *you* owned Sa Virgen. That it was I, and not you, who was the trespasser.'

Held in the strong circle of his hands, Paula looked up at him. 'I don't understand that, either,' she said with an effort. 'But I certainly behaved as though I owned the place. You must have thought me such a savage.'

'I thought you . . .' Again, he seemed unable to find the words. *'Guapissima,'* he finished.

The word made her eyes widen. It meant beautiful or lovely. Then the impossible was true; Juan Torres *did* feel some kind of attraction towards her!

'Why so wide-eyed?' he asked mockingly. 'Haven't you ever been told you're beautiful before?'

Paula shook her head without replying. She looked up at that tanned, ruthless face, her lips slightly parted. Her heart was thudding heavily at the possibility that had just opened before her. She reached up, her hand almost acting on its own impulse, and ran her fingers lightly down his nose, feeling the kink where the strong bone had been broken. 'You wear this like a badge,' she said softly. 'Only I don't know of what.'

'Does it make me ugly?' he asked, his expression intent.

Paula shook her head, her eyes soft. 'Not ugly,' she said.

'Then what?'

Her self-confidence, as though it had exhausted itself in carrying her this far, abruptly seemed to be running out of steam. The enormity of this closeness seemed to have dawned on her.

Suddenly she was afraid—not only of him, but of how strongly she felt about him. Her emotion was too much, too soon. The intimacy they were sharing up in this lonely tower was like warm brandy in her blood, intoxicating her with its sweetness. Her mind was filled with thoughts and desires that alarmed her with their intensity. If she had any sense, she would go now, before another phrase, another caress, captured her any further.

She stepped away from him quickly, and glanced blindly at her watch. 'Is that the time? I've wasted your whole afternoon. I must go!'

His narrowed eyes assessed her. 'You have an appointment?'

'No. I mean, *yes*.' Then, not wanting to lie to him, told the truth. 'No!'

'"No, yes, no",' he mocked. 'I admire a woman who keeps all her options open.'

'I don't have an appointment,' she laughed nervously, dropping her eyes. 'But I—I'd better go, all the same.'

His eyes probed hers for a moment. She knew he was inwardly laughing at her, mocking her confusion. Then he nodded. 'As you wish. We were supposed to be attending to your chignon,' he reminded her. 'What am I supposed to do with it?'

'Oh... Just pin it up any old how. It can't stay like that.'

'A chignon is sophisticated, but a pigtail is girlish?' Juan guessed.

'On me, it is,' she nodded.

'Very well.' He turned her round again. 'How long did you say it had taken you to plait it?' he asked.

'Almost an hour...oh, no!' She yelped, trying to turn round as she realised what the question meant. But it was too late; he'd unravelled half of the plait already, and he continued relentlessly until the thick chestnut hair lay unbraided across her shoulders in a gleaming swathe.

'I should never have trusted you,' she sighed. But Juan was intent on what he was doing. For a moment, the challenging, mocking Juan Torres had become gentle.

'*Dios,*' he murmured, 'such beautiful hair.' He lifted a tress to his lips and inhaled the fragrance. 'And so sweet...' His lowered eyelids lifted to give her a wicked glint. 'Almost an hour, you said?'

'Yes!' she mourned. 'What did you do it for?'

He looked utterly unabashed. 'Firstly, just for the pleasure of seeing it loose. Secondly, allowing for the fact that you couldn't go home like this without raising a lot of awkward questions,' he smiled, 'it gives me an hour more of your company. And thirdly, I shall have the pleasure of watching you do it up again.'

Melted by his reasons, Paula laughed softly. 'I thought I was the one who had a way with words. Well, I can't do it here. Can we go back into the house?'

'Of course. One of the maids will help you.'

Back in the house, Juan summoned the pleasant-faced young maid who had first poured them coffee. 'Do you remember how Señorita Castle's hair was arranged when she arrived?' he asked her.

'Yes, Don Juan.' The sparkle in her eyes told Paula exactly what conclusion she had drawn from Paula's unravelled hair. There was no way, apart from a dignified bearing, of contradicting that impression, either!

'Could you rearrange it in the same way?'

'Yes, Don Juan.'

'Estrella is very skilful,' he assured Paula. 'Why not just relax, and let her do it for you?'

'I'd be grateful,' Paula nodded, and smiled at the maid, who led her to a chair by the window.

Juan went to the row of crystal sherry-decanters on the sideboard. '*Fino* or *oloroso*?'

'*Oloroso*, please,' Paula requested. She hated dry sherry, which to her tasted like diluted vinegar. He poured her a generous measure of the rich, golden wine, and sat near her to watch while the maid began plaiting her hair with deft fingers.

'About that meeting,' Paula said, keeping her head still for Estrella's benefit. 'I've been thinking hard about it.'

He looked weary. 'And?'

'It's likely that the press and television will be there. It could work out to your benefit, you know. If you were able to answer questions and reassure people, you'd make your own path a lot easier.'

'Do you really imagine that your meetings and polemics will persuade the Minister of the Environment to block my plans?' he asked with a scornful smile. 'Am I in enough danger to warrant exposing myself to whatever your friends have laid on for me?'

'They don't have anything laid on,' she said impatiently. 'Except questions.' The smile she offered him was like an olive-branch. 'Anyway, you're a formidable opponent to argue with. Who knows? You might even succeed in persuading the hardliners that you're right, after all.'

He shook his head grimly. 'There are people who will never be convinced,' he said flatly.

Paula thought of Barry Lear and his fierce eyes, and mentally agreed. 'You'd be unwise to underestimate that debate, Juan. My friends, as you call them, are very determined. As for persuading the Ministry of the Environment—that's always a possibility.'

'And you? Are you also very determined?'

She thought hard for a long while before answering. 'When I arrived here this afternoon,' she said slowly, 'there was absolutely no doubt in my mind that your plans were all wrong. But since you showed me that model, and explained what you had in mind...I have to admit my ideas have changed.'

'Wonders will never cease,' he said ironically.

'I don't mean that I'm a hundred per cent on your side.' She glanced at him out of the tails of her eyes. 'But I'm not a hundred per cent against you any more. I'm prepared to admit that you might have a case, after all. And I'd really like people to hear what your plans are. Serious people, like Barry Lear and Andrés Peraza.'

'Indeed.' It was hard to tell whether he was agreeing with her opinion or deriding it. But she was serious. Now that she'd seen his village, at least in model form, she was more determined than ever that he should come to the debate. And she had to admit that it would be a near-perfect solution for Juan to persuade the environmentalists that he was right.

A near-perfect solution for her, too; because if that happened, she'd suffer none of the conflict of loyalties which she knew would eventually arise!

While Estrella worked on her hair, she did her best to persuade Juan of her point of view. When the chignon was back in place, she turned to him with her most pleading expression.

'Please come, Juan,' she said simply. 'It would mean a lot to me.'

He shrugged. 'Very well. If it will stop you nagging me.'

'Oh, Juan!' Impulsively, she beamed at him. 'You'll see,' she promised him, 'it'll be a wise decision.'

'I hope so.' Gravely, he turned her round, and she felt his fingers touch her hair. 'There,' he said, 'every strand back in place. Now, since you're so fond of orange trees, how would you like to come and help out with the harvest?'

She turned to face him. 'The harvest?'

'On Saturday. It's our first of the year. We pick only the ripest fruit, so it's quite a light harvest, but it might amuse you to see a number of the idle rich at work.'

'I'd love to come!' she said excitedly.

'Then you must be here very early,' he warned her. 'We start at dawn, and by three o'clock it will all be over.'

'I'll be here at seven,' she vowed. 'I must go,' she went on, wanting to tell Barry and the others the good news. 'It's been a wonderful afternoon.' And without coquetry, she added, 'I look forward to Saturday—very much.'

It was almost twilight as they walked out to her little Fiesta. The tower was casting a long shadow across the garden, and the air was full of birdsong.

'Goodbye, Paula,' he said softly. As he leaned forward, she felt with sudden dizziness that he was going to kiss her lips; but instead his mouth brushed her closed eyelids. 'I, too, have enjoyed this afternoon. I shall think of you until Saturday.'

His hands slid round to the small of her back, drawing her close against him, and his mouth sought hers. Melting against him, Paula closed her eyes. At first she didn't know how to respond to the warm mouth that explored hers so tenderly; but as the blood surged into her veins, her lips parted to admit his tongue, and taste its message of desire. As their kiss deepened, Juan's fingers caressed her cheek, trailed down her neck, gently cupped the yielding sweetness of her breast.

He was so strong. The shoulders she clung to were hard with muscle, and she was aware of strong, lean thighs pressed against hers. Her head was swimming as he released her, his eyes dark with hunger for her. 'Go now,' he said huskily, 'before we do something foolish.'

She was numb as she got into her car, almost too numb to find the ignition. She waved to him, and set off down the drive, her senses still drugged by him. She saw his tall figure in the rear-view mirror, and waved to him again. Then he was walking back to the house, and she was on her way home, wondering whether she was in a dream.

James was out with friends when she got back home, which suited Paula fine, as she couldn't have faced any fraternal teasing right then. She had a few words with her mother in the kitchen, telling her the bare minimum about the afternoon. She was exhausted for some reason, and longing for nothing more than a long soak in the tub, and an early night.

There was so much to think about. She felt like a different woman from the one who'd left this house a few hours ago—as though Juan had left her with some wonderful treasure which she ached to gloat over in privacy.

Saying goodnight to her mother, she turned to go upstairs.

'Oh!' Her mother's exclamation stopped her. 'What a lovely pin! Did you have that when you went out?'

'Pin...?' She reached up to her hair. There was something securing her chignon. She pulled it out, wondering, and looked at the object in her palm. That was what Juan had done when he'd touched her hair.

The pin was pure silver, and antique. Its head was a big, oval pearl, glowing soft and mysterious in its exquisitely worked setting.

She closed her fingers tight around it, feeling something rise up in her throat. 'No,' she said quietly. 'I didn't have it when I went out. Goodnight, Mum.'

Not answering the questions in her mother's wide eyes, Paula went upstairs to her bedroom.

Lying in her bath, later, with her eyes closed, her mind drifted over the events of the day like a butterfly drifting over still water, seeing its own reflection beneath it. It was like watching a film about another woman, about things that could never have happened to her. What *had* happened this afternoon? Nothing. A little talk, a lovely view, a kiss, an invitation to come and pick oranges. Yet she knew, deep inside, that her life had changed today. Nothing was ever going to be the same again.

Getting to know Juan Torres had added a new dimension to her life. Like discovering that you'd lived next to a mountain for years, but had just never noticed it. It put everything else in your life into a sudden new perspective.

How quickly she had changed from seeing him as her enemy to seeing him as . . . as something else entirely. Beneath that tough, daunting façade, she had discovered something else. Something that called to her with overwhelming strength.

She emerged from the bath, her slender body golden-tanned but for the creamier stripes of her bikini. Wrapped in her towel, she sat at her dressing-table, brooding over the pearl pin. He would never have given her something like this casually. The pearl was a message to her, a message to be taken seriously.

Nor would he have said the things he'd said to her at Alcamar if he hadn't meant them. He wasn't that sort of man; didn't need to be, for he could conquer without stooping to deceits.

Yet she remembered that fleeting moment of terror this afternoon, that premonition that what she felt was too much, too soon. Love affairs that started like lightning might not last much longer than a summer storm. What else, though, did she expect? A full-scale romance, on the strength of two brief meetings? Just because she'd found out he liked her, that he wasn't the monster she had believed him to be, did that mean she had to fall in love with the man?

Crazy! Unless such things *could* happen outside books. Maybe it was possible to know, right from the start, that you and a strange man were destined for one another.

Or was that schoolgirl rubbish? The precious thing in her palm seemed to tell her it wasn't. Ever since childhood, Paula had always hated that feeling of waking from a sweet dream to find that none of it was true, that the bright things she'd dreamed of had fled as soon as her eyes opened. Perhaps that was why he'd given it to her—to tell her that it was real, that it had happened. Like coming back with a flower from a magic garden, to prove that you'd really been there.

Well, she was returning to her magic garden on Saturday; and the thought of that was enough to still every doubt, and inflame every hope in her fluttering heart.

A ripple of excitement spread through the Environmental Group at the news of Juan Torres' attendance at the debate. Within a day of her telling them, great activity seemed to have set in, with Julia Symmonds importantly contacting all her friends in the media, and Barry Lear keeping himself very busy arranging the details with Juan Torres' lawyers, looking even more than usually aquiline.

'He's bringing Alfonso Ramirez,' Julia Symmonds told Paula when they next met. 'Only the best lawyer in Majorca.' She pulled a wry face. 'Your Señor Torres has some very influential friends. He's a real Establishment fat-cat.'

'Well,' Paula smiled, thinking of Juan's lean body, and those acres of orange trees, heavy with fruit, 'at least it's a sign that he's taking this debate seriously.'

'That's what Barry said.' Julia looked fierce. 'He'd better take it seriously. This is going to be no walkover for him, Alfonso Ramirez or no Alfonso Ramirez!'

For once, the topic of Sa Virgen just didn't interest Paula. Everything seemed irrelevant to her now, even her work, which she was normally so busy with. Though she was far too conscientious to let anything slide, her work at the office just seemed a way of filling in the time until Saturday, when she would be with Juan again.

Maybe she was falling in love, after all. And if she was, then her life was different already. Because when weighed in the scale with the little pin which she wore in her hair every day, there was nothing in her life—not her work, not Sa Virgen, not even her family—which mattered more.

CHAPTER FIVE

IT WAS glorious weather, the sun already starting to warm the earth when she arrived at Alcamar, at a few minutes past seven on Saturday morning. In the dewy peace of the morning, the harvest was well under way.

The crew was surprisingly small, just Juan and two dozen men and women of various ages, but they wouldn't let her help with the picking. Instead, they gave her one of the huge Pegaso trucks to drive, and she followed the pickers slowly up and down the avenues of trees all morning. Her feet barely reached the pedals, and the heavy steering made her arms ache when it came to the turns, but there was a deep, almost primitive pleasure in participating.

The tangy smell of citrus was sweet in the air, and the sun rose hot and dazzling over the land. Nor had Juan exaggerated when he'd said she would see him at work; there was no distinction between him and his workers, unless it was that he worked harder and talked less. The Majorcan dialect they all spoke was almost too difficult for even her practised ear to follow, but Juan's occasional contributions caused explosions of laughter up and down the lines, and she had little doubt that the humour was of a distinctly earthy kind.

Sitting on the bonnet of the lorry, passing out the goatskin bag of wine to whoever wanted it, Paula watched Juan with dreamy eyes. He moved like a dancer, yet the work he got through was prodigious; by mid-morning the light cotton shirt he wore was so soaked with sweat that it clung to his skin, revealing the hard muscles of his torso. He was disturbingly beautiful, moving among the others like a stallion among the common herd, the tallest and best-made man by far. Just to look at him was to feel something stir inside you; Paula felt with warm shock the desire come over her to touch that slick, bronzed skin with her tongue, and taste the salt of his sweat.

She didn't miss the way the women watched him, either. If it hadn't been for her jealousy, she'd have been amused at the way they managed to get near him; but if he noticed their flashing glances, or the regularity with which they managed to brush his arm with a breast, or his thigh with a hip, he gave no sign of it. His whole being seemed intent on gathering in the golden oranges, and filling the rumbling Pegaso lorries with the fragrant, heavy load.

He came to her for the goatskin bag when they were three-quarters of the way through the harvest, and looked up at her with sparkling eyes.

'Give me a drink, for God's sake! I'm as dry as a bone.'

'I don't know how you keep going,' she said in awe, passing him the bag. 'I'd be dead by now!'

'Then you'd never make it as an *estanciera*.' He raised the bag high and threw back his head, peasant-style, to let the trickle of red wine jet into his mouth. She watched the powerful column of his throat as he drank, the tanned skin shiny with sweat. Through his drenched shirt she could see the hard, dark points of his nipples, the ripple of his stomach-muscles. The smell of his body was musky-male, intoxicating.

'You look happy,' he said, passing her back the bag and wiping his mouth.

'I am happy,' she smiled. 'I haven't been this happy for ages.'

'Good.' He stood with his fists on his hips, and grinned. 'What are you staring at?'

'Oh...' She flushed. 'I was just thinking how different you look from the other times I've seen you. I ought to be shot for calling you one of the idle rich! What you do would kill the average man.'

'You get used to it,' he shrugged. He studied her figure with unashamed interest; she was wearing faded denims and a checked shirt that was rather too tight across the breasts; one of the women had given her a straw hat against the now-fierce sun. 'And you, little Miss English Paula? Today you look different, too.' His dark eyes drifted across her throat to where she'd used his pin to fasten her shirt over her breasts.

'Juan, I don't know what to say about this.' She touched the pearl with her fingertips. She hadn't said anything about the gift until now, though she'd seen his eyes glance at it more than once. 'It's so precious...'

'You don't have to say anything about it,' he smiled. 'It's nothing.'

'It isn't nothing. It's beautiful and valuable, and I cried when I found it.' She looked into his eyes. 'Thank you,' she said quietly.

'It's been in the family a long time.' His expression was wicked. 'That's a lovely spot for it. If it pricks you, can I kiss it better?'

'It won't prick me,' she said with dignity. 'And you're slacking.'

'*Verdad,*' he agreed. 'Maybe you would make an *estanciera* after all.' With a smile, he went back to work, leaving her to dream.

As he'd promised, the work was over by early after-noon. The laden lorries were picked up by professional drivers, and one by one they roared out of the gates, bound for the docks of Palma. Within days they would be in the supermarkets and fruit-shops of mainland Europe. 'A little bit of Majorcan sun,' as Juan com-mented, 'for places where it's still winter.'

A huge lunch had been spread out on trestle-tables under the trees, and suddenly the day had become a fiesta. Watching the tanned, laughing faces of the workers as they ploughed into bowls of *paella* and jugs of fruity *sangria*, Paula had the strangest feeling of not being in the present at all. This was a scene, a whole day, from some earlier century, when pleasures were simpler and more intense, and life was far better than anything the present had to show.

She was starving, and made a pig of herself with mussels and prawns, but Juan hardly ate a thing.

'I'm too hot to feed,' he said, watching her with smoky eyes. 'Too hot and too filthy. That's the nineteenth mussel, by the way. I've been counting. You'll give yourself the *dolor de estómago*.'

'It holds no terrors for me,' she smiled, polishing off her twentieth. 'I can eat more mussels than you could possibly imagine. You must have something, Juan—you've worked like a Trojan.'

'I'll have to have a swim first,' he said, dropping the orange he'd been trying to eat.

'Have you got a pool?' she asked longingly, suddenly aware of her own too-hot skin and damp hair.

A smile gleamed in his eyes. 'I swim in my *estanque*.'

'Oh.' Visions of a crystal-clear, marble-tiled swimming pool vanished. She knew those Majorcan *estanques* of old. Really reservoirs for irrigation, they were the tra-

ditional swimming pools of country people; but for
someone raised on fastidious English notions and anti-
septic city baths, their greenish depths were hardly
inviting.

'Care to join me?' he offered, his face all innocence.

'It's been years since I swam in an *estanque*,' Paula
sighed.

'Does that mean yes or no?'

'It means I'll assess the algae level before I decide,'
she hedged. 'I'll come and see that you don't drown,
anyway.'

'Sometimes,' he said with amusement, 'I wonder which
of us is the nature-lover. ¡*Vamos!*'

They left the table and walked through the citrus
groves to the reservoir. It was huge, a concrete tank in
which *Epoca* could have turned a full circle; and its
waters, as she'd expected, had a distinctly greenish tint.
Deciding that discretion was the better part of cooling
off, Paula perched herself on the edge and contented
herself with dangling her feet in the sun-warmed water.

Juan, still looking amused, stripped without ceremony. For a heart-stopping moment she stared at a
magnificent male body, broad-shouldered and lithe-
waisted, tanned the colour of mahogany. The black briefs
he wore would not have been decent even on Palma's
anything-goes beaches, but she didn't have time to be
too shattered, because he dived cleanly into the water
and set off in a leisurely crawl towards the other end.
Creaming around his tanned shoulders, the water started
to look deliciously inviting.

It was the hottest time of day, and Paula was suddenly
sweltering in her jeans. Could she really bear not to jump
in? It wasn't the water that stopped her, but the thought
that her underwear was even less decent for bathing than

Juan's. But he was now nearly a hundred yards away, and not even looking at her.

The drop of sweat that trickled down her nose clinched it. Swiftly, she hauled off her denims and shirt, and, wearing only her straw hat, a near-transparent bra and a pair of bikini briefs, slipped into the water.

It was an exquisite sensation; the top foot or two was almost blood-temperature from the sun, but deeper down it grew cold and luscious. You could choose to float on the luke-warm surface, or let your legs sink downward until the cold eddies drifted between your thighs, and you could only just see your feet in the green depths. She set off after Juan at a stately breast-stroke, her hat poised gracefully over her nose.

'I thought your scruples might fade,' he smiled as she drew up to him. 'Feeling better?'

'It's heavenly,' she sighed. 'You just have to get used to green water, that's all.'

'The water is perfectly clean. If it was in a lake, instead of an *estanque*, you'd think it wonderful.'

'I still feel let down,' Paula smiled at him from the corners of her eyes. 'Juan Torres in a reservoir! You'll have to build a marble pool some time, or people will start talking.'

'I've swum here since I was a boy,' he scoffed. 'It's far healthier than wrinkling up in those little tubs of chlorine you English call swimming pools.' He paused, incredibly attractive with his black hair sleeked back from his face. 'Of course, you have to watch out for the *renacuajos*.'

'The *renacuajos*?' she echoed dubiously.

'Little animals that live in *estanques*,' he said gravely. 'They're slimy, but sweet. The bite is quite harmless—

nless it gets infected, of course. As a matter of fact, there's one nibbling at your arm now.'

Suddenly becoming aware of something tickling her elbow, she gave a little involuntary scream, and flailed it away. He grinned wickedly at her expression as she examined the culprit—a floating leaf.

'Beast!'

'You obviously need male protection,' he mocked, swimming over to her, 'before a real one gets you.'

'Do they truly exist?' she asked, trying not to sound anxious.

'Not in this *estanque*,' he promised. His arms slid round her, drawing her close. She almost gasped as she felt the contact of their naked stomachs. Juan's hard thighs brushed against hers.

'Mmm,' he said huskily, brushing her neck with his mouth, the way he'd done in the rose-garden, 'you're as smooth and slippery as a *renacuajo* yourself. Did I mention that they're very good to eat?'

She clung to his shoulders, intoxicated by the touch of his strong body in the water. He was so tanned that her fingers were honey-pale against his fine skin; under her palms, the muscles of his body were alive with power.

'Has it been a good harvest?' she asked, trying to look cool and collected, as though a stunningly attractive, near-naked man held her in his arms every other day.

'"Has it been a good harvest",' he mimicked her conversational tone wickedly. 'Who are you trying to kid? I can feel your heart racing like a trapped bird's.'

She slid her hand down over his own heart. Under the hard muscle, it was thudding hard and fast. 'Yours is, too,' she said breathlessly.

'That's because I've been taking some healthy exercise.' His eyes were intent on the rose of her mouth.

'You are beautiful, Paula. All the men were looking at you this morning.'

'And all the women were looking at *you*,' she retorted. 'Don't think I didn't notice. You're very much lord of the manor here. Are you a bit of a despot?'

'Ruthless,' he said softly. 'No woman is safe within a hundred yards of me.'

'Then I'm in the danger zone,' she said with an uneven smile.

'Yes,' he agreed, leaning forward, 'you are.'

His mouth was warm, covering hers possessively. Unheeded, her hat slipped off, and drifted like a flower on the still water. Her body moulded itself hungrily to his, her breasts pressing urgently against his broad chest. In the cool depths, she felt his hips move forward, a slow caress against her loins as his tongue explored her mouth.

The kiss was long and dizzyingly sweet, ending in a hot flame of arousal in her belly. She arched her back as she felt his fingers trail down her spine, cupping her bottom to pull her closer against him.

'Juan,' she whispered, 'I couldn't take my eyes off you this morning.'

'Then you feel the same way I do.'

Her legs parted shyly at his insistent pressure, and she shivered at the caress of his thigh between hers. The arousal at his loins was hard, unashamed. It made her heart turn over inside her to feel how much he wanted her. And yet it wasn't a crude lust, but something infinitely more mature and sophisticated. He smiled, kissing her gently on the face and throat. Cradling her in his arms, they drifted in silence, lost in the nearness of one another.

Until he sighed, looking down at her through half-narrowed, thick lashes. 'They'll be through with lunch soon, and then we'll have to go back.'

Her body was aching for him as they swam to the edge, and hauled themselves out. 'What are we going to dry ourselves with?' she wanted to know.

'We'll have to sit in the sun,' he smiled. 'The crew can wait another ten minutes.'

They sat on the hot concrete by the edge of the pool. His eyes studied her body with brooding passion; she was all too aware that the water had made her underwear all but transparent, and her nipples were as plain to see as rosebuds against gauze. For her part, it was an effort not to let her eyes drop to the swelling black triangle between his thighs.

He kissed her again, his mouth deliberately erotic now, his tongue teasing hers like a flame, so that she moaned, and melted against him. She was unable to resist him; something in his touch drugged her, turning the blood in her veins into molten honey.

'Thank you for coming today,' he said gently.

'I wouldn't have missed it for worlds,' she sighed. 'It's been bliss. I just hope I wasn't in the way too much.'

'You were very helpful. You drove that wagon like a born trucker. You've earned your pay-packet.'

'My pay-packet! I don't want any pay——'

'You must have it,' he grinned. 'Union rules. It's not princely by your standards, but you still shouldn't turn it down.' It had taken barely minutes for the sun to kiss the last droplets from their skins, and he touched her smooth thigh with his fingertips. 'We don't have a reason to kiss any more,' he said regretfully.

'Do we need a reason?' she smiled, her arms linked round his neck in delicious possession.

'We need a good one,' he sighed. 'I have to pay my crew now, or I won't be lord of the manor much longer. Then I have to get down to the docks to arrange the shipping. And then,' he winced, 'I have a cocktail party to go to.'

'With Cristina,' she guessed, her eyes clouding.

For a moment he looked as though he were going to deny it, but then he nodded. 'With Cristina.'

At least he wasn't looking forward to it, she thought, her jealousy stinging like a nettle. 'Does Cristina ever swim in the *estanque* with you?' she asked sweetly.

'What do you think?'

'I think she'd be too frightened of *renacuajos*,' Paula volunteered.

His soft chuckle was a reward. 'The *renacuajos* are frightened of her, more likely. But to answer your question, I think Cris would rather melt in the sun than put her little toe in an *estanque*. Come, sweet one. We must go.'

At least this was one place where she hadn't been preceded by Cristina Colom, Paula thought as she buttoned her shirt. But the other woman's name had intruded into this paradise like an unwelcome guest. She didn't know Juan well enough to press him about her; she had no justification for doing so, anyway. A few kisses gave her no rights over him.

But she'd dearly love to know how things stood between Juan and Cristina. She cared too much about him not to wonder. She didn't want to be just a flirtation for him. She wanted to be more, much more than that. Her feelings about him were intense enough to warn her that she stood to be hurt very badly indeed if anything went wrong; and Juan consorting with Cristina Colom definitely came under the category of things going wrong.

Was it going to end here? What if he didn't want to see her again? The sudden thought of going home without another appointment to see Juan Torres was like a pain in the heart.

He caught her troubled gaze on him, and quirked an eyebrow. 'What's bothering you?'

'Nothing,' she lied, smoothing her face out hastily.

'Have I offended you?' he asked, tilting his head at the *estanque*. 'In there, I mean?'

'No.' He was just wearing jeans, and she nestled up against his warm, bare chest. 'No,' she repeated softly, 'you haven't offended me in the slightest.'

'Good.' He kissed her firmly, then laced his fingers through hers. 'There isn't another harvest for weeks,' he said gravely, 'and I've agreed to come to your debate on the twenty-ninth. What excuse do we have for seeing each other now?'

The pain in her heart melted into joy. 'You think of one,' she invited with an appearance of calm.

'Have you got a head for heights?'

'They don't bother me.'

'Then would you like to come for a ramble on Puigpunyent with me?' he asked. 'I don't mean a serious climb, just a walk to look at the wild flowers—and maybe see one or two of those eagles you're so crazy about.'

'I'd love that,' she exclaimed. Puigpunyent was the highest peak on Majorca, and one of the most wildly beautiful areas of the island. The last time she'd been there was with a school party, years ago, and she'd never forgotten it.

'How about tomorrow?'

'Perfect!' This time, she didn't try and hide her pleasure, and he was amused by her eagerness.

'Good. You can drive us. My old Ferrari doesn't like mountain tracks.'

'Then you ought to buy yourself a jeep,' she said. 'I'm beginning to suspect you of being stingy, Don Juan.'

'Jeeps, marble swimming-pools,' he sighed. 'I'm just an orange farmer, girl. Come on. Let's get back to the real world.'

The days that followed were the most blissfully happy of Paula's life. High on the peaks of Puigpunyent with Juan Torres, or on the walks and swims that followed, she seemed to leave everything behind her, and become a different woman. Happiness was deep inside her, a joy in being alive and being in love that was almost transcendental.

His knowledge of nature exceeded hers. He knew the names of all the wild plants, and he had a countryman's knowledge of which were good to eat, which had medicinal effects, and which were poisonous. He was an extraordinary man, she began to realise; a mixture of strength and intellect that was very rare. Sexually and physically, he was almost brutally male, but there were reserves of sweetness and humour in his character, like pools among rocks, that she delighted to taste. Her need for him was like wine in her veins, filling her with sensations she could only half understand.

At first James and her parents teased her about the amount of time she was spending with her 'enemy'; but as they saw the light in her eyes and the dreamy beauty that had fallen over her like a magic spell, they stopped making jokes, and looked at each other knowingly instead.

Their curiosity was rampant. A more than gentle hint was dropped to the effect that it was about time she brought Juan Torres to meet them.

He had asked her out to dinner on the Thursday before the public debate, and had arranged to pick her up from home at seven, and that seemed an appropriate time for her to introduce her family to him.

She chose to wear her green velvet dress, the only item of evening wear in her wardrobe that could really be called stunning. Cut low across the shoulders, it showed her beautiful throat and arms off perfectly, and her breasts were full enough to make it distinctly sexy. Set off with a satin belt around her slim waist, the lustrous material brought out the full richness of her colouring without seeming too obtrusive.

The pearl pin required a little thought. She was leaving her hair down tonight, because she knew he loved to see it loose. She thought of wearing it like a brooch until it occurred to her that Juan would certainly bring her a corsage. That was an old Majorcan custom—and anyway, he was just that sort of man. She could use the pearl pin to fasten the flower to her dress. She slipped it into her bag with a smile.

Her mind returned to yesterday, to the exquisite golden afternoon on the beach. They hadn't kissed, the way they increasingly did, but had just lain in each other's arms in the lee of a sand-dune, talking for hours in the soft, intimate tones of lovers.

What had they found to talk about for three long hours? There had been so much to say that it was difficult to remember whether even a fraction of it had been said. And yet now she was bursting with more things to tell him, knowing that she would explode into a happy babble as soon as she saw him . . .

Her father whistled in admiration as she came down the stairs with her little velvet evening-bag, and her light wool cape slung over one arm.

'I say,' he marvelled, 'you mean business!'

'Yes,' she agreed, smiling, 'I mean business.'

'Poor devil,' he commiserated with the absent Juan. 'He doesn't stand a chance.'

'You look lovely, sweetheart.' Her mother's eyes were proud and warm. She had guessed far more than the others what Paula's state of mind had been over the past few days. 'Absolutely lovely.'

James' contribution was, 'Shouldn't you be plastered with make-up?'

Paula shook her head. She was wearing the same minimal touches as she'd worn last week, feeling instinctively that Juan was not a man to admire an elaborate job of face-painting. Her lips had been glossed, and she had emphasised her eyes with kohl and a touch of shadow, but that was all. She had the sense to know when she looked her best, as she did now.

And at that moment, the rumble of a car outside heralded Juan's arrival. James, at the window with the evening paper, looked out inquisitively. 'Wow! Some car!'

'Do we kiss his hand, or just genuflect?' her father grinned.

'Be nice, everyone,' she pleaded with her family hurriedly, making for the door. 'I'll go and fetch him in.'

It was one of those magical spring nights that felt like summer. The thousand lights that danced on the water of the Bay of Palma were scarcely as bright as the stars, which shone down from a sky of the deepest, velvety blue. She'd never been to Las Anclas before. Like

everyone else in Palma, of course, she had heard about
it. It was a long way out of the financial reach of the
boys who usually took her out, even if they'd had the
clout to get past the beribboned porter outside the stone
portals. Situated on the glamorous Paseo Maritimo, the
famous restaurant overlooked the yacht marina, a view
as fabulous as anything Monte Carlo or Biarritz had to
show. And whatever the meal might have cost tonight,
it was among the best Paula had ever eaten, and she said
so.

'You've already said that twice,' Juan smiled at her.

'Do I sound gauche? It's just that I usually don't in-
dulge myself with food. But oh, I do love it!'

'I shall have to make sure you don't get fat, in that
case.' His dark eyes drifted to her breast, where his orchid
nestled against her dress, fastened by the pearl pin. 'That
would be vandalism of an even worse kind. However,
there seems to be no immediate danger. That dress suits
you, Paula.'

'It's not too daring?' Paula glanced round at the extremely formally dressed diners around them. 'I didn't
realise that Las Anclas was the "appropriate place" you
had in mind—or I'd have hired a fur!'

'It's not too daring. You have a beautiful body, and
you should show it off.' His eyes glittered. 'Within
reason, of course.'

She smiled at him, too shy to tell him how stunning
he looked. If there had ever been a special male devil
made to tempt women into folly, he would have looked
something like Juan Torres tonight, Paula thought. It
was the combination of suave refinement and raw male
power that was so magnetic. The evening suit added a
veneer of sophistication, but any female eye could discern
the tiger's body beneath the beautifully cut black silk.

And, in fact, not a woman in this restaurant tonight had failed to look at Juan with that half-disguised longing which would either have infuriated or depressed their companions, according to type.

But Juan's eyes had barely left her through the whole course of the meal. The attention was intoxicating, as well as deeply flattering. Sitting opposite him was like sitting before a hot fire; he seemed to radiate warmth and excitement, and she was soaking it in without reservations.

'Thank you for being so charming to my family,' she said, dropping her eyes from his. 'You enchanted them.'

'They enchanted me. I liked them very much. And they obviously adore you.'

'They like to tease me,' she said ruefully. 'Especially James. I was dreading that they'd start tonight—and I couldn't have borne it, not in front of you!'

'I don't think they'd be that tactless,' Juan smiled. 'Elder brothers aren't all bad. I have some experience of younger sisters myself.'

'Does Isabella look like you?'

'In colouring? Yes. You can tell we're brother and sister. However,' he added drily, 'her nose isn't broken.'

Paula looked at his face. 'Does it worry you?' she asked gently.

He smiled and shrugged. 'It worries other people more, I think.'

'You could always...' She hesitated delicately, not knowing whether she was stepping out of line.

'Get it straightened?' he supplied for her. She nodded. 'Yes, I could. I will, one day.'

'One day? Why not now?'

Juan laughed softly. 'Are you that keen to see me restructured?'

'Your face doesn't put me off, if that's what you mean. In fact——' She tilted her chestnut head to one side, eyes sparkling. 'I don't know whether I don't prefer you like that. With your nose straightened you might be too beautiful for your own good.'

'I presume that's a compliment of some sort,' he grinned. 'However, I agree a dented nose does have its advantages. It can make you look very fierce.' He narrowed his eyes at her as he spoke, and the effect was so chilling that she reached out impulsively.

'Don't,' she begged. 'God, I'd hate it if you were ever angry enough with me to *really* look like that!'

'Then stay in line.' He nodded at her plate. 'Too much for you?'

Paula looked ruefully at her lobster thermidor. It was utterly delicious, but so huge that she'd only been able to manage half of it. 'I'm very much afraid so,' she sighed. 'And I know I'll curse myself tomorrow.'

'Nonsense. Take it back with you.' A glance from Juan had the waiter bustling over. A few brief instructions, and Paula's lobster was whisked away, to be returned a few minutes later, exquisitely wrapped in foil and tied with a silk bow.

'Wow—that's service,' she smiled. But she didn't kid herself for one moment that the attentions of the staff were anything to do with her. It was her host—called by everyone 'Don Juan'—who commanded the deferential treatment. And not just because he was paying the bill. That 'Don Juan' said a lot. There wasn't a real equivalent in English for the title 'Don'; it implied friendship, but also profound respect. And it was never given to foreigners.

Here at Las Anclas, where rich and famous guests were commonplace, Juan Torres was accorded the kind of respect which could only come from belonging to one of the island's oldest and most respected families. She had seen that look of respect and affection on other faces, too, even on the face of the policeman who had stepped out of his *coche-patrulla* to greet Juan on the Paseo Maritimo, earlier tonight.

It was slightly intoxicating, Paula had to admit, to be with the kind of man whose presence was an event wherever he went. It wasn't just summoning waiters with a tilt of one eyebrow, or having policemen get out of their squad-cars to say *buenas tardes*. It was having the kind of personality that others found magnetic. In an ancient time, she had no doubt, Juan Torres would have made the kind of charismatic leader who ruled tribes and clans.

'You're dreaming,' he reminded her with a smile.

'Sorry.' She took her stare away from him, and shook herself out of her reverie. 'I was far away.'

'Very flattering. I'm going to have a glass of brandy— will you join me?'

'It wouldn't be wise. But I'll love watching you have one.' She propped her chin on her interlaced fingers, and looked at him with softly smiling eyes. 'Are you going to have one of those special affairs with the little flame under the glass?'

'*Cielo*, no.' He looked amused at her obvious disappointment. 'Why?'

'I'd love to see you go through the ritual. *And* have a cigar, a Cuban one the size of a stick of dynamite.' With lordly aplomb, Paula went through the motions of selecting a cigar from an invisible humidor, snipping the end off, and lighting it with elaborate puffs and snorts.

Juan exploded into laughter at the pantomime. 'Little actress! Do such things impress you?'

'Ceremonial suits you,' she said simply. 'It was invented for people like you. You're the only man I've ever known who could do things like that, and look marvellous, instead of pompous. Will you at least do it with the brandy? For me?'

'If you'll join me.'

'Right, and to hell with being wise,' she capitulated.

Another glance from Juan had the waiter back at their table. With considerable ceremony, two huge brandy balloons were brought, each one poised over a tiny flame on a silver carriage.

'To you.' Juan swirled the amber liquid in her glass, and passed it to her.

'To you,' she repeated, lost in his eyes. The fuming Majorcan brandy was fiery, rushing straight to her head and making her lean back with shining eyes. 'Whew!'

'Now you know what it's like on the other side of the ceremonial,' he smiled.

She looked into her glass. It was a measure of truly royal proportions. 'Golly, that's some glassful.'

'The cellarman will be spending tomorrow scribbling in his books,' he agreed. 'Don't let it get cold.'

'Juan, I don't think I can drink it, after all!'

'Ah!' His eyes were mock-melancholy. 'Not to finish one's brandy is an unforgivable insult to one's host on Majorca.'

'Oh!' Taking a deep breath, Paula gulped down the whole more-than-generous measure. It was hardly like liquid at all, more like a kind of running fire that rushed down her throat and surged back up to her brain in almost the same instant. There was the sort of whoosh in her ears that petrol makes, when thrown on a bonfire.

From a long way away she heard his voice saying, 'You're supposed to sip it steadily, Paula.' Juan was obviously having to hide his smile at her flushed cheeks and throat. 'Aren't you glad you don't have to light a cigar now?'

'I think the top of my head would blow off,' she said huskily. The room was swimming around her, and she could hear her own heart pounding. She replaced the glass with elaborate care in the carriage, and sat up very straight. 'Juan,' she said conversationally, 'if I don't get out into the fresh air, I'm going to faint.'

He was at her side in an instant, helping her to her feet, and snapping his fingers for her cape.

'Come,' he said, 'let's take a walk along the quay.'

'The bill...'

'The bill will be sent to Alcamar.' He escorted her smoothly out past the bowing staff, murmuring his appreciation of the meal to the manager, and then they were out in the cool dark.

CHAPTER SIX

THE fresh sea-breeze was delicious on her flaming cheeks and throat, and Paula gulped it down with closed eyes. The waves of giddiness subsided slowly, leaving her with an ethereal, floating feeling, as if her feet were an inch or two off the ground.

Juan's strong arm was around her waist, holding her close to his side. With a sigh of sheer, unadulterated bliss, she let her head rest on his shoulder. 'You're the most wonderful man I've ever met,' she said dreamily.

'Paula——'

'I'm sorry I was such a little bitch on Sa Virgen. Only I didn't know...'

'Paula, have you ever had brandy before?'

'Never.' With an effort, she picked up her head, and focused on his face. 'Does it show?'

'Only to someone who knows you very well,' he said solemnly. 'Let's walk.'

'I'm heavy,' she warned, aware that he was more than half supporting her.

'Oh, I think I'll manage.'

'You're so strong.' She snuggled against him again, pillowing her cheek against his shoulder. Her feet didn't seem to be walking, more gliding along beneath her. 'I love Palma. I love Majorca. I love...'

'Look at the boats,' he interrupted gently. 'Where's *Sulky Susan* moored?'

'Right at the other end, with the serious boats. All this,' she said, waving at the huge yachts moored alongside, 'is frivolous stuff.'

'Ah,' he said. 'You disapprove of this end?'

'Not really. I love all boats.' She stared dreamily at the hundreds of ghostly masts in the moonlight. The distant hum of traffic blended with the murmur of yachts' lines tap-tapping in the gentle breeze. It was deeply peaceful. She wanted to stop and drink it all in, but he forced her to keep walking down the quayside, by the edge of the lapping water.

'I wish we were on Sa Virgen right now,' she whispered. 'Just you and me, on the cliff.'

She caught the glint of his teeth. 'Have you ever been there at night?'

'No.'

'It's wonderful. We'll go, you and I, some night soon.'

'And spend the night there?'

'Yes.'

'Promise?'

'I don't need to promise.'

'Promise!' she demanded fiercely, afraid that he might be teasing her. She swung round in front of him to stop him, and stared up into his face again. The thousand lights that danced on the bay were reflected in his eyes, making them even deeper and more mysterious. 'Please, Juan...'

She was not pleading about Sa Virgen any more. He took her in his arms, and their lips were brushing suddenly, gentle as moth's wings, exploring, caressing one another's faces. Juan whispered her name as his arms tightened around her. The world about them seemed to vanish as he kissed her mouth long and hard. She was hungry for his tongue, shuddering as it entered her mouth to touch her own. Paula felt her body melting against him, her breasts crushed to his chest; languorously, she reached up to touch his cheek and temple, then ran her hand slowly through his thick, crisp hair, feeling the springy curls wind themselves around her fingers.

Their kiss seemed to deepen, as though they were plummeting through ocean depths. There was nothing real but their caressing tongues, the velvety feel of lips and the intoxicating proximity of one another's bodies. Kissing had never been like this. This was a communion of souls. They said more to each other with their lips and tongues than they could have said with a thousand words; revealed more about their feelings and desires than a year of love-letters could have done.

It was only the low murmur of voices that parted them. A little group of strollers was passing by along the quay, their faces indulgently turned the other way. Paula's breath was ragged, her pulses leaping in her throat. She felt drugged, but not by the brandy any more.

Somewhere in the town, a distant clocktower chimed eleven, followed by another, further off.

'I'm sober now,' she said in a low voice. 'Did I make a complete fool of myself in Las Anclas?'

'Nobody noticed a thing,' he said. He was outwardly calm, but there was something in his eyes and voice that made her shudder with re-awakened passion.

'I've never been kissed in public like that,' she whispered.

'What a dull life you must lead,' he smiled, caressing Paula's throat with his fingertips.

'Don't,' she shivered, trapping his hand between her own. 'Juan, you frighten me! I've never felt like this.'

'I must remember to give you brandy every time we go out,' he said gravely, slipping his free arm around her slender waist.

'There are going to be lots of times, then?' she enquired. 'I'd die if I thought you were just amusing yourself with me!'

'That's the brandy talking,' he decided, nudging her into a walk again. 'And stop being so insecure.'

'Easy for you to talk about insecurity,' she sighed. 'You're so special, and I'm so ordinary.'

'Not exactly ordinary,' he said drily. 'Or are you wanting me to lather you with compliments?'

'That's not your style,' Paula agreed. 'But I just...' Her voice tailed off.

'I'm not playing with you, Paula.' For a second time they had stopped, this time at his insistence. His eyes searched deep into hers. 'I'm not that sort of man. I'm not going to tell you exactly what I feel about you, because firstly this isn't the place, and secondly, your head is still swimming with brandy. But I can assure you that my feelings are no less serious than your own.'

Paula smiled hesitantly. 'My feelings are very confused, Juan...'

'Of course they are. Now stop worrying,' he commanded. 'You're too romantic for your own good!'

He steered the conversation gently on to other topics as they continued their stroll. He seemed to know the owners of practically all the hugest and most dazzling yachts in the harbour, and he made a deliciously amusing raconteur. She was still laughing at one of his stories as a sleek, familiar grey shape caught her eye.

'Oh, look—there's *Epoca*!' He nodded, and Paula tugged him towards where the beautiful launch was

moored. 'You're so lucky,' she sighed, looking up at the
boat, starry-eyed. 'She's magnificent.'

'You like her?'

'When I first saw her in Cala Vibora, I hated her,'
Paula confessed. 'She looked so aggressive and
expensive!'

'She's both,' Juan nodded with a hint of irony.

'Show me round,' she pleaded. 'I'm dying to see what
she's like inside.'

'I thought you'd already had a good look,' he reminded her. 'Through your binoculars.'

'Not a good enough look! I want to see it properly.'

'At this time of night?'

'The time of night has nothing to do with it!'

'My grandmother would never have approved,' he
smiled. 'A man and a woman alone on a boat, late at
night—*and* without a chaperon.'

'You were alone with Cristina Colom the other week,'
Paula pointed out wickedly. 'And I didn't notice any
chaperon through my binoculars—unless you had one
hidden in that bottle of champagne.'

'Your binoculars must be sharper than I thought,' he
said, unperturbed.

'Please,' she smiled. 'James would never forgive me
if I didn't go aboard—he's even madder about boats
than I am. I know it must be absolutely fabulous...'

'I suppose it is. Very well.' Pulling off his dinner-
jacket, he gave it to her to hold, then swung himself
easily on board. Holding his still-warm jacket, she
watched the gleam of his silk shirt moving in the
darkness. Then the boarding-ladder swung smoothly out
towards her, and she climbed up on to the deck.

A bulkhead lamp filled the seating area with light,
and Paula found herself standing amid a symphony of

grey. The soft charcoal carpet underfoot was definitely wool, after all, and a touch confirmed that the luxurious seats were upholstered in the finest hide. 'Wow!' she breathed, and inhaled the rich smells of leather and fine wood. 'Who fitted her out?'

'Seaways International, in Poole,' he said, naming one of the best boatyards in England. 'Come up on to the bridge.'

She followed up to the highest point of the yacht, where a small sunbathing-deck was protected by immaculate canvas screens. The wheel was set in a spacious cockpit, canopied by backswept perspex, and surrounded by a bank of dials and screens.

'Do you know anything about navigation equipment?' Juan asked, and when she shook her head, he gave her a brief explanation of how the computerised navigation system worked. 'In essence, you could navigate from here to America without consulting a chart once,' he smiled. 'Want to see the cabins?'

'Yes!'

A companionway led below to the deceptively spacious under-deck area. There were two double cabins leading off from a neat lounge and galley. He took her into the larger one first, which was beautiful enough to make her gasp.

The soft cream wool carpet was literally ankle-deep underfoot. Its sophisticated shade exactly matched the walls, which were upholstered in the finest padded calfskin. The ceiling was leather, too, dark blue spangled with tiny gold stars.

Pearly concealed lights made the mahogany gleam where miraculously skilled craftsmen had built in cupboards, shelves, a dressing-table and a velvet seat. The metal of the oblong portholes looked as though it might be gold-plated. Over the bed was a large oil-painting, a life-size female nude whose dark eyes challenged Paula with a mysterious smile. The bed itself was vast and low, and when Paula sank on to it, yielded deliciously under her slight weight.

'My God!' she sighed.

'Is this to your taste?' he enquired, tilting one eyebrow to her.

'It's totally decadent,' she smiled, looking up at him, 'outrageously luxurious and absolutely indefensible. I love it.' She sank back on to the bed, slim arms stretched out above her head, and gazed dreamily up at the gold-starred ceiling. 'Can I take it home with me?'

'I never suspected you of such sybaritic tastes.' He moved to sit beside her, and leaned over her, smoothing the tumbled chestnut hair away from her face. 'I thought you were so resolutely Spartan about boats.'

'Oh, I could grow to like this kind of thing. In fact, I think I'm being corrupted.'

'Don't tell me you think money automatically means corruption?'

'My friends think you're an Establishment fat-cat,' she smiled.

His eyes narrowed to black slits. 'A fat-cat? What the hell does that mean?'

'It's an American word. It means one of those rich, sleek men who grind the faces of the poor. Let me think of a Spanish equivalent. Ummm...*un cacique*. An exploiter.'

'A capitalist hyena?' he suggested, lifting one eyebrow.

'That kind of thing,' she giggled.

'Ah.' He looked relieved. 'Nothing to do with my figure, then.'

'There's nothing wrong with your figure.' Paula looked up into his eyes, feeling her senses stir at his proximity. 'Thank you for tonight, Juan. I've loved every minute of it.'

'I'm glad.' He bent down to kiss her mouth. Her lips clung to his as though reluctant to let him escape, but he wasn't letting the kiss develop into anything. He drew back and smiled down at her, and Paula reached up to touch his cheek.

'Do you think I'm too young for you?' she asked softly.

'A little,' he nodded, still smiling. 'Why do you ask?'

'You hold back sometimes.' She hesitated. 'When you're touching me, or kissing me. As though you wanted to go on, but stopped yourself. *Verdad?*'

'*Verdad,*' he agreed solemnly. 'It's difficult, but I do it.'

'I wish you wouldn't,' she said, colouring as she uttered the words. 'Sometimes.'

'Oh?' White teeth glittered in his smile. 'The lamb is asking for the wolf to be let past the gate?'

'I'm not exactly a lamb, Juan.'

'You are,' he contradicted gently. 'Exactly a lamb. And as a responsible wolf, I have to be wise with you.'

'I threw wisdom to the winds tonight, when I drank that brandy,' she said, tracing the shape of his warm mouth with delicate fingertips. 'Why don't you do the same?'

'Paula, Paula,' he said softly, eyes narrowing to smoky slits, 'I half believe you led me here tonight with the sole purpose of seducing me.'

'I'd love to seduce you,' she said with a little laugh that caught in her throat. 'If only I knew how.'

He trapped her hand and kissed the slim, tapering fingers. 'Seduction is an art that takes a long time to learn, *querida*.'

'A long time.' Her parted lips were soft, shamelessly inviting. 'That sounds nice.'

'The skills are difficult.' He kissed the inside of her wrist, where the pulses were beating fast and unevenly now. 'The practice needed is long and arduous.'

'I'll have the advantage of a good teacher,' she whispered. 'And I'll promise to try and be a good ... pupil.'

'A good pupil.' Juan's dark eyes glittered down at her. 'So you're not put off by the long hours or the hard work?'

Paula shook her head. Looking up into that beautiful, brutal face, she knew in her heart that she would never feel about another man the way she felt about Juan Torres. She didn't need words to tell him that; he could see it in her own eyes, feel it in her pounding heart, so close to his...

Slowly, he drew his forefinger down the line of her throat, down her breastbone, to the top of her velvet dress. 'You're so beautiful,' he said dreamily. He turned the velvet back so that her naked breasts were revealed to his intent gaze, the perfectly shaped nipples rising from her firm flesh proudly. 'So beautiful...'

This time there was no holding back in his kiss. It was unlike any of their previous kisses, unlike anything she'd known before. This time there was a fierce passion in Juan that overwhelmed her. His mouth mastered her, his tongue tormenting her senses until she moaned against his lips, and arched against him, her fingers fumbling with the buttons of his shirt.

His skin was like velvet under her palms, hot and musky. As he cupped her breasts, teasing her nipples into hard points of desire, Paula felt all shyness leave her. There could be no reserve with a man like Juan. It had not occurred to her until a minute ago that they might make love tonight. She'd never given the possibility more than a dim thought. Yet now, faced with the heat of his commitment, there was neither turning back, nor the desire to turn back.

It was in the spontaneous furnace of such passion, she thought numbly, that the half-formed clay of human impulses was either seared into perfection or burst into wasted fragments. Yet she had not lied when she'd said she wasn't afraid. She wanted him too much, hungered for him with an urgency that allowed of no deviation.

At first their kisses were long and slow, like the elaborate, deliberately formal dances that opened a ball. But as her arousal peaked under the assault of his expertise, her caresses became more feverish, more demanding.

Impatiently, he pulled his shirt off, and she reached for his body with hunger. Under her caressing palms, the dark nipples were hard with desire against the bronzed flesh. His skin was hot, the muscles tense with anticipation.

'Your beautiful dress is getting crumpled,' he said huskily. Dizzily, Paula watched the muscles ripple and pulse as he took her dress off completely, laying it across the chair with as much tenderness as though it were a part of her he was touching.

All she wore beneath it was a pair of lacy briefs, and when he took her in his arms again, the contact of their naked skins was like an electric shock. To touch him was unbelievably erotic. Juan's body was utterly different from her own, so hard and strong that, though she'd always thought of herself as firm and fit, she now seemed a creature of delicacy and softness beside him.

And for his part, her woman's body seemed to intoxicate him. He murmured in wonder as he traced the graceful lines of her figure; the delicate arch of a bone, the curve of smooth flesh, the living rosebuds of her nipples, all seemed to fill him with a deep tenderness. He used his mouth and hands as though worshipping her, as though she were the first woman he'd ever made love to.

Paula had never dreamed that lovemaking could mean anything like this; like any normal woman, she'd been aroused by men before, had discovered feelings of tenderness and desire in herself. But this was a world away from such pale experiences. It wasn't just that Juan Torres was a wonderful, sensitive lover, who had the experience to make her feel sensations beyond her dreaming; it was the man himself, the proud, noble spirit of the mate who was now choosing her, whose heart was pounding so close against hers as their mouths met.

She was liquid with readiness when at last his caresses reached the inner secrets of her womanhood, her whole body as tense as the fullest flower-bud, waiting to explode into blossom. Her own hands found him, learned his manhood, the touch of her fingers against his burning flesh drawing a deep gasp from him.

It was intoxicating to touch him like this, to be touched in return, their caresses expressing a trust, a desire, that went deeper than any casual sex could ever go. Did he understand that she was a virgin, that this was the first time for her? Somehow, it didn't really matter. As she caressed his desire, her hands filled with the proud manhood that would soon be within her, taking her from one phase of her life into a new one, she felt in her heart that it didn't matter. Had she lost her virginity a hundred times, this would still have been the first real love-making she'd known.

And nothing could have made him a gentler, sexier, more wonderful lover than he was being now.

If the gods willed it, there was a new life waiting for her beyond this ecstasy, a life that would be flooded with Juan's presence, just as his lovemaking was flooding her now.

So she said nothing, just whispered his name, again and again. There would be time to tell him, later, if he didn't already know.

The touch of his fingers between her thighs was an ache, a delicious torment that was never quite enough, never taking her to the edge of that explosion into blossom her soul yearned for.

'*Querido,*' she said, her voice ragged, 'don't make me wait any longer, I beg of you...'

His laugh was husky, his eyes deeply tender as he looked down at her. 'How unwise are we being?' he asked softly. 'I mean, have you thought of the consequences of what we're doing?'

'The consequences? Oh...' Paula smiled shakily. 'It's perfectly safe right now, my love.'

He tilted a sceptical eyebrow at her. '*Famosas últimas palabras,*' he growled. 'Nothing is *perfectly* safe, young lady, especially not that kind of Russian roulette.'

Desperate not to spoil it all, she shook her head. 'There won't be any consequences.'

'You sound very sure.' He kissed her clinging lips. 'Are you...protected?'

'Yes,' she said, closing her eyes so he wouldn't see the lie. 'Come to me. *Please!*'

Her desire couldn't wait a second longer; and as though her urgency had ignited his, he slid between her thighs with a moan, his hands cupping her face as his mouth found hers.

It was as though the whole of Paula's life had concentrated itself in that one moment. Lying beneath him, her womanhood offered to his passion, her maidenhood inviting its own destruction, she felt a profound wave of love for him wash through her being.

It was strange and wonderful to feel him deep inside her, and she was numbly aware of the salt tears spilling across her cheeks and on to the pillow.

'*Preciosa,*' he whispered, kissing the tears with gentle lips. '*Estoy enamorado de ti.*'

'*Yo también.*' Her voice was unsteady. '*Estoy enamorada de ti, Juan.*' She looked up into his face, her beautiful eyes still shiny-wet with tears. There had been no resistance, no tearing of flesh, only the long, slow thrust of his desire that culminated in this moment of utter communion. She was conscious of a great beauty, as though that flowering she'd ached for were already here.

When he began to move within her, it was so carefully and gently that she barely felt it at first. But the feeling changed, grew, became a surging flood of pleasure that was different from the sharp delights of their first touching, yet far deeper. Her whole body seemed caught up in it, every fibre, every muscle taking up the rhythm that locked them together. Primal, elemental, Juan's lovemaking was a forceful act of creation.

She was lost in his speed and power, chained to his desire like a sail filled by a hurricane. There could be no holding back, none of the deliberate teasing that had gone before. He wanted her too much, and she exulted in that want. Rising in magnificent power to a peak, their act of love pulsed headlong towards the first shuddering moments of its conclusion. And as Paula's helpless body started to arc in an unbelievable spasm of pleasure, she felt with aching clarity the scalding flood of his seed inside her.

The aftermath was like drifting high above the clouds, pillowed in his arms. It seemed like hours later when the first hints of reality crept into her senses—the cool touch of air on her moist skin, the distant lapping of water against the yacht's side, the murmur of Juan's voice telling her not to cry.

'S-sorry.' Clumsily, she dried her eyes. 'I won't always be like this.'

'I never want you any different.' He smiled down at her, brushing the tumbled hair out of her face. 'You were talking pure Spanish all the way through. Did you know?'

'No.' She laughed shakily. 'I'm surprised I had the breath to talk at all, in any language.'

He drew her close and kissed her. 'You're wonderful,' he whispered. 'I've never known a woman like you.' She lay in his arms, dreamily blissful, listening to him tell her things she'd never dreamed to hear from this man. With an inner smile it occurred to her that he hadn't guessed at her virginity yet. Well...was that a compliment, or otherwise? Imagining his face when she told him made the smile spread to her lips. She'd always know that her first time would be without much pain or drama; she was just made that way. But as for her long-held feeling that it would be an anticlimax——!

A long time later, Juan reached out for his gold Rolex, and winced. 'It's one o'clock in the morning. Are your parents going to be waiting up for you?'

'I think they've given up worrying about me.'

'Oh?' he enquired dangerously. 'You make a habit of staying out till one in the morning?'

'No,' she admitted wryly. For the first time in her life, she was regretting that she lived at home. It would be so natural, so marvellous to spend the night on this yacht, with Juan. 'Maybe I should get back before too much longer.' She sat up slowly, pulling her hair back with weak arms. 'I feel as though I've just run a fifty-mile marathon...'

'There's an electric shower in there,' he smiled. 'I think we can both squeeze into it. Will you join me?'

It was somehow natural that showering together took far longer than necessary, and involved a mutual exploration of each other's slippery bodies that almost led to making love a second time. She emerged before him, giggling and naked, and bundled herself into the luxuriously thick towel.

Catching sight of herself in the full-length mirror across the cabin, Paula stopped. Did she look any different? Her body was the same, tanned and firm, highbreasted and long-legged; but her face—yes, that was different. There was something in the eyes, a kind of silent laughter, that had never been there before. Juan came behind her, shaking water from his hair.

'Such vanity,' he murmured, kissing her naked shoulder.

'Not vanity,' she smiled, suddenly acutely shy. 'I just wanted to see if your lovemaking showed.'

'You are as beautiful as a flower. That is what shows.' He took the towel out of her hands, and came to stand next to her, so that they were both reflected in the mirror their nakedness side by side. 'Are we well matched?'

'I think so.' They were beautiful; his height and breadth made her femininity look exquisitely fragile, and she in turn revealed the majesty of his male strength. She could have stared at the image for hours, lost in the wonder of what had happened to her, but he kissed her cheek and slapped her bare bottom lightly.

'Come, *querida*. We must go—it's very late. Your father will shoot me.'

She reached up to kiss him. 'I don't care if he shoots us both. This is the happiest night of my life!'

Driving home through the empty streets of Palma in the open Ferrari was deliciously magical. The old car had been designed exactly for occasions like this. Nestled up against him, she gazed with dreamy eyes on the moonlit palm-trees, the silent moonlit *avenidas* ...

She felt completely at one with Juan, locked in an intimate world where only the two of them existed or mattered.

'What are you thinking of so intently?' he asked, caressing her cheek.

'You,' Paula smiled. Strangers to lovers, she thought. The transition had been so swift, barely a few weeks. Yet it had also been so inevitable. It had been written, from the start, that this was to happen. If only it lasted! The only spectre to haunt her happiness was the fear of being left by Juan.

He'd said his feelings about her were serious. Yet she knew enough about men to know that they could say one thing before making love, another thing afterwards. It wasn't necessarily deceit; it was something in the way they were made—an inherent lack of a woman's constancy. Filled with desire for a woman's body, many a man had fancied himself in love—to discover once the act was accomplished that the emotion was considerably lessened.

Ugly thought.

Had he made love to Cristina Colom, on that same bed, the day they'd met? Another thought which made her shiver unhappily, as though a cold wind had just eddied through her heart. The memory of Cristina's black eyes was chilling, accusing. They seemed to call her usurper, traitress.

She remembered with a pang what Cristina had said on Sa Virgen: *I know she's amusing and pretty, but you've wasted enough time with her.* Was that the way it really was? A diversion for Juan Torres while his fiancée was in Paris for a week or two? After all, she was the alien here. Juan and Cristina were both Spaniards, probably old friends. Both were rich, both came from the very cream of Majorcan society. And by his own admission, he'd been considering marriage to Cristina.

What had he said? That Cristina had beauty, considerable wealth, and shared Paula's opinion that Alcamar needed a woman's touch.

Ah, no... She should have kept on dreaming. It wasn't advisable to consider her true scale in Juan Torres' life. What could he, a rich, important man, want with a girl like her? Her love for him was a fantasy, a spring eccentricity on which it would be crazy to place any reliance.

Yet she couldn't help the way she felt. Her love for him was its own justification. It came with its own hopes, its own dreams, its own folly.

When he spoke, however, it was clear that his own thoughts had been revolving along very different lines.

'You're coming to this debate tomorrow, of course?'

'Front row seat—I wouldn't miss it for worlds,' she said, forcing herself to sound cheery. 'The whole of Palma is going to be there.'

'Your friend Barry Lear is certainly determined to make a spectacle out of it,' Juan replied thoughtfully. 'He tends to treat this very emotively.'

'Barry feels deeply,' she shrugged, nestling closer.

'Yes,' Juan said drily. 'But what does he feel so deeply—love of nature? Or hatred of people?'

'Hmmm. Cynical question.'

'I don't like him.'

'I do. He's an honest man who feels very strongly about the environment. He's committed. And he's a real expert on Majorcan falcons, you know.'

'Big deal,' Juan snorted.

'You don't respect any of them, do you?' Paula said indignantly. 'You can be so scathing about conservationists!'

'And you can be very over-impressed by them,' he retorted. 'Lear sets himself up as an expert, but his knowledge is all out of books. He can tell you to the last mouse how many rodents the average falcon eats in a year, or to the millimetre what the average egg-size is. But he can't set a broken wing, or cure a sick hawk.'

'How do you know?' she demanded, sitting up.

'My uncle, Emilio Torres, is a *real* expert on falcons. He's a falconer, like my grandfather, and my great-grandfather. There's one at least in every generation of our family. And Barry Lear has to go to *him* with his sick or injured birds.' Juan gave her a wicked smile. 'It's like swallowing poison for Lear. He detests Emilio, because Emilio knows more about falcons than he'll ever know. And going to him for help is admitting that Emilio is the better man.'

'Hawking is cruel,' was the only retort Paula could think of. 'It's not much better than bullfighting.'

'Like life,' Juan nodded, 'hawking is both cruel and beautiful. So is bullfighting. And both are deeply ingrained in Spanish culture.'

'You *surely* don't approve of bullfighting?' she asked, wide-eyed.

'I neither approve nor disapprove. I don't have enough arrogance to do either.' He glanced at her. 'And please don't tell me that it's cruel and savage and primitive. I know all that. But I also know that it goes far back into the very roots of my people, and that Spain would be a poorer country without it.'

Paula snorted. 'Funny how all blood-sports are regarded as cultural treasures. The English are the same about fox-hunting.'

'In any case,' he smiled, 'what are you lecturing *me* for? I assure you that bullfighting is not to my taste in the slightest. Nor is fox-hunting. But hawking, now— ah, Paula, that is a beautiful pastime. To unleash the falcon from your wrist, and see her fly like a thunderbolt into a blue summer's sky... *that* is beauty.'

'Pagan,' she said darkly, but he only laughed at her.

'Well, I don't share your admiration for Barry Lear— or his friend Peraza, for that matter. They are both men with a chip on their shoulders. Their fanaticism leads them into decisions which honourable men would shun.'

'Such as?' she challenged.

'Such as invading Sa Virgen last year with their gang of freaks.'

'They had nothing to do with that,' Paula assured him. 'It wasn't a very good idea to begin with, but it would have been all right if things had worked out the way they were meant to. The trouble was that a whole lot of outsiders got involved, people who didn't really care about the environment at all. There are always lunatics on the fringe of any organisation, Juan—what you call "freaks". Don't confuse them with people who understand and care about the real issues at stake!'

They had reached her house, and he parked under the big lemon trees and turned to her. 'Don't let's quarrel,' he said softly. 'Tonight has meant too much to me.'

'And to me!' Instantly melted, Paula slid into his arms, putting up her mouth to be kissed. It was a long, sweet kiss, reminding her so intensely of what had happened between them earlier tonight that she was trembling when he released her.

'It's obviously way past your bedtime,' he said firmly, getting out. He walked her to the door, his arm tight around her waist. Under the portico, he took her face in his hands, kissing her mouth long and tenderly. 'Now,' he said huskily, 'go and get your beauty sleep.'

'Juan——' She wanted to say something, to tell him in some way how wonderful this night had been for her, what it had meant to her. But he silenced her lips with another kiss.

'Don't say anything. This isn't the time. And I know everything you want to say. Go!'

She let herself into the sleeping house, kissed him once through the door, and waited in the silent darkness, eyes closed.

When the rumble of the vintage car had faded in the night, she went slowly upstairs to bed.

God! What a night...

The unexpectedness of what had happened was starting to make her mind reel. She was no longer a virgin, no longer an unattached girl, but a mature woman, fully in love with a man. And what a man... As she lay in her narrow bed, she ached for the warmth of Juan's embrace, her mind plundering the treasury of exquisite memories it had stored up. It had been an incredibly romantic evening. Not in the sense of pink clouds and silver bells; Juan's lovemaking had been too earthy and physical for that!

But the true romance of the occasion had been inside them, in their hearts. If she could have scheduled the way she wanted to be made love to for the first time, it would have been exactly like that; an initiation into dizzying physical pleasure without pain, embarrassment or clumsiness.

But much, much more than that, a blinding discovery of how much rich emotion there was to making love. The way her girlfriends sometimes talked about it made you think it was a purely physical thing. It wasn't. It was the tangible expression of a spiritual passion that went far, far deeper.

Learning about what your body could feel was also learning about what your soul could feel. In love, the two were one, indivisible and inviolate...

She didn't resume her afterthoughts in the car. They were for another time, another place. Right now, she just wanted to be with Juan, in her imagination if not in reality.

But sleep came in like a thief, stealing away her memories, replacing them with dreams that were sometimes blissful, sometimes confused, sometimes shadowed with fear.

CHAPTER SEVEN

SHE'D never seen the Ramón Lull Hall so crowded. It wasn't just the large throng in the auditorium; there were at least three separate television crews around the stage, adding to the confusion with microphones and dazzling lights. The atmosphere was excited, but also tense. Anticipation was in the air like an electric current.

The Environmental Group were present in force, naturally; but Paula recognised or half-recognised other faces, too, people she hadn't seen for months. It was a significantly large turn-out for a topic of relatively low public interest.

'This reminds me of my student days,' James said, sitting down beside her in the front row, where she'd reserved two seats for them. 'Some of the people here look pretty wild. I hope your Juan has some experience in handling crowds.'

'He'll manage,' Paula clipped out. Though she tried to hide it from her brother, there was a tight ring of pain in her stomach, and she felt slightly ill with nerves. Odd how she'd never actually given a thought to how this night was going to turn out. She'd just assumed it would be an orderly, peaceful debate, in which Juan Torres' natural authority would shine like a beacon.

But surrounded by the reality of this excited crowd, faced with the confusion of the media crews gathered round the long table on the stage, and waiting for the entrance of the central figures in the debate that was to unfold, Paula felt her confidence evaporating. Suddenly she was very glad that James had insisted on escorting her to the debate, and was sitting beside her with his usual vague smile in place.

What if the debate didn't go Juan's way? What if he were defeated and humiliated here tonight? What if the end result of tonight's performance was that Juan was in fact stopped from building on Sa Virgen?

That didn't bear thinking about. Oh, idiot Paula! She'd been so caught up in the passion of falling in love with him that such thoughts hadn't even dawned on her stupid mind!

'Who did the artwork?' James asked, casting a glance up at the big poster hanging behind the stage.

'Looks like Julia Symmonds' work.' It was emotive, rather than beautiful, a deliberately raw painting of a dead falcon lying in a pool of blood. Why was a self-proclaimed nature-lover like Julia, Paula thought absently, so fond of painting animal blood? She shouldn't have been allowed to hang a thing like that over what was meant to be a serious, dispassionate debate.

Nor did she think the choice of slogan, 'Hands off Sa Virgen', particularly apt. That was going to remind too many people of the stupid 'invasion' last year.

'A general shortage of good taste all round,' James said approvingly. 'That's what I like to see—barbed wire and barricades.'

'Very funny.' Paula heaved a brief sigh. What in God's name had made her so sanguine about getting Juan to this meeting? If things went wrong she'd never forgive herself. She'd been so anti-Juan a few short weeks ago. Was she on the other side now? She wanted to see fair play, at any rate. Oh, Juan...

A burst of loud laughter from behind tore into Paula's reverie. The voices of the crowd had risen to a continuous rumble all around. She could only pray that the rowdy element weren't going to be here tonight.

There was a burst of scattered applause—and some jeering—as the protagonists arrived, and the table started to fill up. The television lights were turned full on them. Barry Lear, in casual clothes, was looking tight-faced and tense. With him, as always, was Andrés Peraza, and a group which included at least two well-known scientists.

Juan, one of the last to arrive, was head and shoulders above the rest in height. Wearing a formal dark suit, Paula thought he looked magnificent. He was expressionless, as he often was in public, and beside him was a robust, middle-aged man with silvered hair, who must be Alfonso Ramirez. With them were three or four other legal-looking people. One of them, Paula recognised, was the Proyecto Virgen spokesman who'd attended debates like this in the past. She saw Juan glance up at the huge poster overhead, but it didn't seem to bother him. Ramirez was carrying a briefcase, Juan was empty-handed.

There were shouts from the back of the hall as they came in, but in the general confusion Paula couldn't make out the words, just an ugly animal noise.

Finally, the man from the Department of the Environment arrived, smiling politely through the hubbub. He was accompanied by an efficient-looking female secretary with a notepad.

'Here we go,' James murmured to Paula. She nodded, pale-faced. She only had eyes for Juan; but apart from one brief nod in their direction, he appeared to ignore them completely, listening instead to whatever it was his lawyer was saying in his ear.

The table was arranged in a V, with Juan and his party on the right, and the environmentalists on the left. At the point of the V was Léon Iglesias, the chairman of the meeting, and an experienced public speaker. When he eventually stood up to ask for order, the noise subsided at once. With a brief introduction of Juan, the Ministry man, and some of the others, including Barry, he declared the debate open. It was to begin with questions from the table; later, he promised, the discussion would be open to questions from the floor.

The first question was scheduled to Barry Lear. His eagle eyes intent, he launched into a long attack in his terrible Spanish, directed at Juan. The rambling accusations and insults went on for so long that Léon Iglesias eventually interrupted to ask what the question was. A thunderous burst of applause, however, indicated that it had been well-received by at least some of the audience.

When Juan began to answer a silence fell that was absolute. His clear, deep voice could not have been a greater contrast to Barry Lear's excited gabble, and the calm assurance he radiated began to untangle the knotted nerves around Paula's heart. He was so logical, answering Barry's questions with such obvious honesty that Paula felt no one in the hall could have been unconvinced.

There was loud applause as he finished, but some booing, too. As the next questioner, an ornithologist, began speaking, Paula turned to her brother and whispered, 'Was he all right?'

'I thought he was splendid,' James nodded. Glancing at his sister's pale, tense face, he added gently, 'You really care about him, don't you?'

Paula just nodded, her attention fixed on the stage. Juan was answering in the same cool way, expressing his concern that the birdlife of the island should not be disturbed, and giving his assurance that everything would be done to protect it.

There was a shout of *'¡Mentiroso!'* from the back of the hall. Juan glanced calmly in that direction.

'I am not a liar,' he said quietly. 'Any of you here who know my name will know that I may be many things—but not a liar.'

There was laughter and applause. The next question, from another scientist, was long and technical. The man from the Ministry, who had been looking interested up till now, began to show signs of sleepiness, and Paula felt with considerable relief that the tension was ebbing out of the crowd.

'It's going to be all right,' she said quietly to James, who nodded and smiled.

In fact, the next hour strengthened Juan Torres' case considerably. He and Alfonso Ramirez continued to answer questions patiently and directly, and Paula sensed that the common opinion had swung steadily their way. At least two of the scientists had expressed themselves satisfied that, so long as Juan stuck to his promises, there was no real threat to the ecology of the island.

In a sense, that brought her intense relief; she'd come round to the same opinion herself, but it was good to hear it confirmed by experts. She felt in her heart now that Juan's plans for Sa Virgen were right and just, and that there could be no more objections.

Barry, however, was looking very black. She remembered Juan's judgement, that he would never be convinced. But Juan's arguments were so strong, his intentions so plainly excellent, and so well-expressed, that she felt no crowd could have failed to be swayed.

There was an element that she hadn't reckoned on, too; so many of the opponents of the Proyecto Virgen

scheme seemed to be foreigners, and the sympathies of
the Majorcan audience were clearly loyal towards Juan
Torres. Indeed, the only signs of antagonism so far had
been between members of the public.

In fact, when questions were finally invited from the
floor, the atmosphere grew swiftly rowdier. Two or three
of the questioners verged on the abusive, and Paula could
hear shouts and what sounded like scuffles from behind.

Her nerves returned in full force. Craning her neck to
see over the people behind her, she caught sight of a
grim-faced knot of young people in the centre of the
hall. They looked scruffy and long-haired, but also purposeful. A big, red-faced girl in the middle of them was
on her feet, haranguing Juan, shaking her fist as the
accusations spilled from her mouth. The lunatic fringe,
she thought with a sinking feeling. She'd so hoped they
wouldn't be here tonight. She ought to have known that
this was exactly the kind of opportunity they loved.

What happened next she couldn't clearly follow, but
someone from the crowd seemed to get up and push the
red-faced girl, who collapsed backwards with a piercing
shriek. Suddenly, a brawl had broken out. Fists were
flying amid a flurry of denim and leather jackets, and
two or three women screamed in fright.

Like everyone else, Paula was on her feet now. Léon
Iglesias was shouting for order, but no one paid any attention. She looked helplessly at Juan, whose expression
had not altered.

Then the first missile sailed through the air, landing
with a crash beside the table. Stunned, Paula registered
that it was a bottle.

The man from the *Ministerio*, who had been looking
pleasantly refreshed after his nap, got to his feet, and
started hustling his secretary towards the exit. The at-

mosphere was utterly changed. Evil was in the air, and fear, too. The fight had spread outward, and it was hard to tell who was intent on aggression, and who was simply trying to get out of the way.

Part of the audience had started chanting, led by the red-faced girl; raucous and in poor Spanish, but orchestrated: *'Sa Virgen por los halcóns! No volemos cabróns!'* That was what they'd chanted on Sa Virgen last year. There was a sudden flush of crudely painted banners, too, waving like battle-flags. Where had they been until now? Bottles were flying towards the stage, so many that she knew with horror that they had been deliberately brought for the purpose. The air was full of the sound of breaking glass, and she saw a cameraman reel from his machine, shaking a blood-spattered hand.

With a cry, she tried to scramble up the stairs towards Juan, with some confused idea of protecting him, but James grabbed her swiftly, and huddled down with her in the chair.

'Keep your head down,' he said urgently, sheltering her face with his jacket. 'This won't last long.'

She struggled to get free, but James was too strong. Glass shattered nearby, and she flinched. She was whispering, 'Oh God, oh God,' without even knowing it. From under James' sheltering arm, she caught a glimpse of someone flailing a banner wildly, using the post as a weapon. It seemed for sickening minutes like a full-scale riot.

Then there was a lull in the bottle-throwing, and James cautiously eased his grip on her. The scruffy-looking contingent were marching on the stage with their banners, chanting savagely; everyone else seemed either to be cowering out of the way, or to have left the hall. The stage was a shambles of milling people, overturned chairs and broken glass. The government man and his secretary were nowhere to be seen, and nor was Juan.

Until a knot of people moved aside, and she saw Alfonso Ramirez kneeling over the figure who was sprawled among the overturned chairs. Physical sickness hit her like a blow as she registered that the motionless body was Juan's.

Blood had soaked his shirt and suit. He was very white, barely breathing, and the handkerchief Ramirez was trying to staunch the wound on his head with was a sodden red ball.

Paula's legs were suddenly like rubber things that could not support her weight, and folded beneath her. Numbly aware that her body was collapsing like a marionette whose strings had been cut, she crumpled to the floor, a wave of blackness darkening her vision.

James caught her as she fell, and stopped her from sprawling headlong among the broken glass. For a while, there was only a roaring void in which voices and footsteps echoed weirdly with strange music. Slowly, she slipped back into consciousness feeling deathly sick, and weak to the bone.

'Juan,' she moaned, lifting her head to peer through tumbled hair.

'Are you all right?' James demanded. He looked into her eyes with unsympathetic professionalism. 'A good old Victorian faint, nothing more. You'll probably vomit,' he warned her, wiping her clammy brow.

'Juan's hurt——'

'I know,' he nodded, 'I've seen him. I'm going to get my bag from the car. OK?'

She nodded, and blundered through the crowd to find Juan. She found him by catching sight of Alfonso Ramirez's silvered hair among the confusion. He was still vainly trying to mop the blood away from Juan's face, and as she got up to them she saw the welling gash in Juan's now-clotted hair.

'Dear God,' she whimpered, sinking to her knees beside him, and cupping his face in her hands, 'are you all right?'

He didn't move, and as she embraced him, his powerful body was as limp as death.

It was a nightmare. It couldn't have happened. It was impossible that such violence could have erupted without warning. Oh, where was James? There were police uniforms in the hall now, dispersing the milling crowd. She registered blood in evidence on other faces and shirt-fronts.

The brutes, the *savages*!

'He's concussed,' the lawyer said helplessly.

'My brother's a doctor. He's just fetching his medical bag—he'll be here any moment.' She wiped the useless tears away from her eyes. 'Juan! Can you hear me?'

'It was deliberate.' Ramirez looked anguished. 'I saw the young man aim the bottle from just there—a few metres away. I could do nothing! *Dios*, they might have killed him!'

At last James came hurrying back from the car with his medical bag, and knelt at her side, examining Juan critically. 'Nasty,' he muttered. 'He's out cold. I don't like that.'

'What can you do?' Ramirez asked.

'Right here and now, not much,' James said. 'The police have called an ambulance, which will be here in a few minutes. I'll clean the wound and take a look at the damage in the meantime. Put his head in your lap, Paula.'

Carefully, Paula lifted Juan's head on to her lap, oblivious to the blood that swiftly soaked into her once-beautiful white suit, and cradled his motionless shoulders in her arms.

Pulling disinfectant and his instrument-case from his bag, James started carefully probing the gash in Juan's head.

Fighting down her emotions, Paula looked away. The hall was a battlefield of overturned chairs and abandoned possessions. At the far end, the police were hustling the last of the chanting mob out. By the looks of it, at least one had been arrested. Only one camera crew was left intact, but they were filming avidly, the bright eyes of their spotlights sweeping the horrible scene.

She looked back down at Juan. Under the deep tan, the handsome face was pale as ivory, his long lashes closed. 'Is he badly hurt?' she asked James helplessly.

'He'll need an X-ray to tell that. Ah!' He looked pleased. 'Got a big piece of glass out. If he's lucky, he should get off with a stinking headache. His head seems hard enough, anyway. OK, it seems clean. I'll disinfect. Can you make a circular pad, the way I taught you?'

Paula nodded, taking the bandage he passed her, and started folding it. Concerned-looking policemen had joined the group around them now. As she pressed the pad carefully round the wound, holding Juan's head gently against her breast as she did so, it occurred to her that she'd been part of the agency that had hurt him. What a criminal fool she had been! His blood was on her hands. Literally. His hurt was her fault, all of it. If he died, she would be to blame.

The thought was utterly appalling. Please God, let her stupidity not have killed him!

'How is he?'

She registered that the voice was Barry Lear's. He was watching Juan with an expression of concern. 'Is he going to be all right, doctor?'

'I don't know,' James said briefly. 'You've got some very destructive friends, Mr Lear.'

'They were not friends of mine,' Barry replied calmly. 'I can only feel sorrow at the whole incident. It's most regrettable.'

' "Regrettable"?' Paula echoed. 'It's more than that!'

'I'm afraid people lost their heads,' Barry said coolly. 'They let their frustration and anger get the better of them. That is regrettable.'

'It's a shocking business,' the senior policeman agreed grimly. 'Don Juan is a good man. This should never have happened.'

'I'd be extremely sorry if he's been seriously injured,' Barry said gravely.

His eye caught Paula's as he spoke, and she saw with shock the dry, cynical glint in it. God! How could he be such a vicious hypocrite? He felt neither regret nor sorrow about what had happened.

In fact...

The thought that dawned on her was so monstrous that at first she discarded it. But she couldn't get a sentence out of her mind, a sentence Juan had once spoken: 'Their fanaticism leads them into decisions which honourable men would shun.' Had this been planned? Any of it? *All* of it?

God! What if Juan had been right? What if she was enmeshed in a plot...

She glanced at the policeman, then at Barry. Did you do it? she asked with her eyes. His returning gaze was cold, yellow, expressionless. The merciless stare of a hawk. There was no information in it, no answer to the silent question she sent to him.

James, oblivious to any of the unspoken exchange between Paula and Barry, had been taking Juan's pulse, and was now peering thoughtfully into his eyes with his ophthalmoscope. 'I don't think there's any haemorrhaging,' he decided. 'Cerebral concussion, almost certainly, but probably no fracture.'

'The ambulance has arrived,' a policeman hurried up to tell them. 'They're bringing a stretcher.'

'Good.' James nodded, and smiled at Paula. 'You'll have to give him up now, sis.'

The ambulancemen took Juan's weight off her lap, loaded him expertly on to the stretcher, and hustled his blanket-covered form towards the exit. Then he was gone. Panic rose up in her as she watched the stretchermen disappear. What if he died?

'Can we go with him to the hospital?' she asked James urgently.

'You won't see much of him. He'll go straight to X-ray, and then to intensive care—or possibly a theatre.'

'I want to go, all the same!'

'OK.' James nodded soothingly, catching the note of desperation in her voice. 'We'll follow in your car.' He glanced down the hall. There was still chaos in the main foyer. 'We'd better go backstage and find one of the stage-doors.'

They pushed behind the curtain and followed the exit signs down a maze of dingy corridors until they reached an unlocked fire-door.

As they emerged into a twilight alleyway, they both froze in their tracks. The street was deserted. But parked just a few yards down was Juan's Ferrari. Or what was left of it.

It had been pounded with clubs or iron rods until not a panel was intact. Fresh horror broke on her as she registered the shattered windscreens, the long, gleaming red bonnet that was now a mass of dents, the door that hung like a broken wing. As she took a numb step forward, she saw that the leather seat where she'd sat on the night they'd made love had been ripped open with a knife, its stuffing spilling obscenely out.

'Oh, bloody hell!' James groaned. 'As if they haven't done enough.'

'Mad,' Paula whispered, staring at the devastated car with empty eyes. 'They're mad!'

'Wait here. I'm going to call the police.'

She nodded, and he went back into the hall. A slogan had been spray-painted along the side of the car, but she didn't even try to decipher it. She felt sickened to her soul, as though tonight's proceedings had been a kind of horrible violation, blow upon blow.

Footsteps sounded behind her. But when she turned round, it wasn't James. It was Barry Lear, his hands in his pockets. The bearded, aquiline face wore a gentle smile.

'Well, well,' he said, surveying the wreckage of the once-lovely old car. 'Shame about the Ferrari.'

There was something in the yellow eyes, a sardonic amusement, that ignited fury in Paula.

'You put those thugs up to this!' she said in a low, shaking voice.

'Did I?' he asked coolly. 'That's quite an assumption.' He kicked gently at the broken glass around his feet. 'I call this a shocking act of vandalism. Of course, to some people it would be a legitimate act of protest against a rich and powerful menace to society. But that's just an opinion.'

At that moment, any remaining doubt left her mind.
The whole cruel business had been scheduled. She was
now utterly certain that Barry and others had planned
this débâcle, right from the start. They'd meant everything to happen exactly as it had happened. And she,
stupid, gullible she, had been the lynch-pin of the whole
plan.

She could only stare at him as though hypnotised, her
skin cold as ice. 'You're mad!'

Barry looked at her with a glitter. 'I told you we'd
give him something to think about, didn't I?'

'And *this* is what you meant?' She sagged against the
cold stone wall. 'God, Barry, I can't believe it! You don't
know what you've done. After what happened on Sa
Virgen last year...' She shook her head dumbly at the
enormity of it. 'Don't you realise that you may have
killed him?'

He looked at her consideringly, as cool as though
neither the riot back in the hall, nor the destruction of
the car, had meant very much to him. 'Who's this
"you"? I had nothing to do with any of this.'

'Liar!'

'Don't you remember me shouting for order?' He
smiled. 'I was very brave. Several people have already
said so.' He cocked his head on one side, madly birdlike,
and studied her white face. 'Besides, it's over now. Why
not forget the nastiness and try to remember what this
has all been about?'

'I think I've forgotten,' she said with bitter irony.
'What *was* it all about?'

'It's about the world we have to live in.' The first hint
of passion appeared in his eyes and voice. 'It's about
people who are too rich and well protected to be got at
any other way. It's about the defenceless birds and plants

on Sa Virgen which are going to be crushed under Gucci loafers and Range Rover tyres unless someone does something.'

' "Does something"?' she echoed incredulously. 'You call this helping the cause of conservation? You're a criminal, Barry. You ought to be locked up!'

His considering stare hardened. 'I knew you didn't have it in you. You're not really committed, Paula. That's why you weren't told what would happen. You're a spoiled little bourgeoise—and don't think I don't know you're half in love with Torres. Everyone knows. It's written all over your face.'

'I can't understand *why*,' Paula said quietly. 'What in God's name makes you think this is anything but a disaster—for us, for Sa Virgen, for everything?'

'Majorca is an island of hoteliers,' he said brusquely. 'That's why there's never been any real opposition to Juan Torres, and people like him. Everyone's too damned keen on making their own pile to want to interfere with anyone else making *his*. They're not going to stop until the whole Mediterranean is one hideous concrete block, with not a plant growing except in hotel gardens, not a living thing in the sea except tourists, and not a bird in the sky!' He paused for breath, his face set and hard. 'The authorities are hand-in-glove with the developers, Paula. It's they who are mad, not us. They're money-mad, profit-mad, hotel-mad!'

She could only shake her head, starting to be more than a little afraid of him. The thread of truth in his words only made the rest of it seem all the more deranged.

'We have to show that the *people* are against it,' he said, more quietly. 'The ordinary people, not rich bastards like Torres and his like. When this hits the headlines tomorrow, it'll be a signal. A war-cry. A call to ordinary people, showing them that they *can* show their opposition, that someone has dared to stand up to the establishment and strike a blow. We won't just be a lot of cranks any more, Paula. We'll be a *cause*.'

'If I tell the police what you've just told me——' Paula began in a shaky voice, but he cut through sneeringly.

'You're hysterical,' he said contemptuously. 'I'll deny it. Everyone will deny it. It was a spontaneous outburst of popular feeling. They'll never believe you, girl.'

'They might just,' Paula said, dark-eyed with pain.

'And if they did?' he smirked. 'You'd be in it up to your pretty little neck.'

'What do you mean?'

'I mean that you got him here,' Barry retorted. 'If there was any plan, you're part of it. And you'll go down with everyone else, I guarantee it.' The sound of footsteps made him glance quickly over his shoulder. 'So keep your mouth shut, Paula. For your own good.'

James had returned with two policemen in tow, and in silence she watched them examine the car, Barry acting out well-feigned shock. Disbelief was still numbing her. Her world had collapsed around her. This was her fault. The fault of her stupidity, her gullibility, her criminal thoughtlessness. Everything that had happened tonight had hinged on her, the way a gun hinged on a trigger. Staring with unseeing eyes at the ruined car, she felt like walking straight down to the harbour and stepping off the pier into oblivion. The poison of her guilt was eating into her soul.

What was she to do with the horrible knowledge she now carried inside her? Speak out, tell these policemen that Barry Lear had planned the whole thing? But how could she tell the truth about Barry without implicating herself? And she had no evidence, not even a proper admission from Barry. She glanced at the policemen, but didn't even know where to begin. God, what was she going to do?

Barry's eyes met hers across the alley, and the expression in them changed to one of such malignant threat that she huddled defensively into her coat. He wasn't just a common criminal, whose viciousness deserved punishment. He was a dangerous fanatic who might do anything in the name of his cause. He was crazy, she thought distantly. This was the man she'd respected! This madman was the person whose integrity she'd placed so much reliance on!

'*Señorita!*' One of the police came up to her in concern. 'Are you hurt?'

Following his gaze, Paula looked down at her white suit. There was a large bloodstain where Juan's head had lain. 'No,' she said dully. 'It's Señor Torres' blood. I'm all right. Thank you.'

'Your brother has given us your names,' he said gently. 'There is no need for you to stay here. It would be best if you went home and tried to relax, now. You look very shaken.'

'Good advice,' Barry said smoothly. 'Why not take your sister home, Dr Castle? She's had a nasty shock.'

'They're right.' James brushed the heavy chestnut hair away from her face. 'There's nothing more we can do here, sis. Let's get to the car, go home, and have a cup of tea. Then, later on, I'll take you across to the hospital to check up on Juan. OK?'

'OK,' she whispered. It was like moving in a dream. Exhaustion and grief had sapped her strength. She sagged against James wearily, who put a comforting arm around her as he led her away.

'He'll be all right, Paula. You'll see. It'll all be all right.'

CHAPTER EIGHT

THEIR parents had seen a newsflash of the riot on television, and were in a state of quiet desperation by the time they got back; and Paula's mother's nerves weren't improved by seeing Paula arrive covered in blood.

But the trip to the hospital later that night proved fruitless. Juan was still being X-rayed at midnight, and James, looking at Paula's drawn face and dark-ringed eyes, insisted that she go back home again and try to sleep.

When she awoke the next morning at ten, feeling completely shattered, there was more news for her.

'The X-rays are good,' James informed her, putting a cup of tea at her bedside. 'I have that from the horse's mouth. No fractures, and no haemorrhage.'

'Thank God.' She sat up blearily, struggling to focus her exhausted mind. 'Is he going to be all right?'

'According to my contact, yes. He's had stitches, of course, but the scar's under the hairline,' James smiled, 'so unless he goes bald, it won't show. Apart from that kink in his conk, he's the beautiful animal he always was.'

'And he'll be discharged?'

'Probably tomorrow. They say he'll be able to see visitors this afternoon. Want to go?' Her look made him laugh. 'OK. I'll take you this afternoon. I've brought you the papers. You might find them interesting.'

The Ramón Lull riot had made the front page in all three morning editions. One of them carried a picture

147

of Paula sitting with Juan's head in her lap, surrounded by policemen. Even the most radical of the papers had condemned the attack as an outrage, and although it had given prominence to an interview with Andrés Peraza, trying to steer attention back to the issue of Sa Virgen, Paula had the distinct feeling that the plan was going to backfire on Barry Lear & Co.

She read the reports over her tea, then stared out of the window, feeling a cold wave of fear trickle through her veins. What kind of reception was she going to get at the hospital this afternoon? Juan would have every right to blame her for what had happened. Could she ever manage to persuade him that she hadn't deliberately lured him into that murderous trap? Seen through his eyes, how ugly it all might seem. It didn't bear thinking about.

She rose and dressed, then set about trying to wash the blood off her white skirt of last night. It was a futile task; the stain was obstinate, and her fingers were nerveless. Right now, she couldn't have felt much worse if one of those bottles had hit her, instead of Juan. Maybe she'd have felt better, indeed, less tormented by guilt.

She loved him so much...

He was a part of her already. If he were to walk out of her life right now, it would tear a great ragged hole that would be very hard to heal. This stranger, this lover, who had suffered hurt through her own stupidity, was suddenly the most important thing in her universe. Like a once-free planet, she'd been harnessed by the gravity of a new sun; and if that sun were to go out, she'd be left spinning into chaos, alone.

James used his contacts at the hospital to get her on to the ward at two, a full hour before visiting officially started. The point was to miss the crowd of people that would no doubt have arrived to see Juan Torres by three.

Knowing she would want to be alone with Juan, James left her in the foyer, and went off to find some cronies in the doctor's canteen.

But when Paula got to the top floor, another visitor had preceded her.

A slim, elegant woman emerged from the private room where Juan was staying, closed the door firmly behind her, and barred Paula's way. Paula met the cold, black eyes of Cristina Colom, and felt her heart sink into icy depths.

The other woman stared at her for a long moment, the strangely animal quality of her beauty emphasised by the expression of contempt on her face.

'I tried to warn him against you,' she said quietly, but with intense feeling. 'He would not listen. Perhaps he will listen now. What have you come here for? To look at the damage you've done?'

'I've come to see Juan.' Her voice was tight. 'The matron told me he was awake.'

Cristina smiled without humour. 'You think Juan wants to see you? Your insolence is almost amusing!'

'Please let me by,' Paula said tersely.

Cristina's eyes flicked over Paula's clothes. She was perhaps only five or six years older than Paula, but there was a world of difference between the poise and style of the Spanish woman and Paula's fresh innocence. The sort of difference that great wealth and great arrogance can make.

'The matron is wrong,' Cristina said flatly. 'He is sleeping. You cannot go in.'

'Then I'll wait,' Paula replied coolly.

'In which case I can impart a few home truths,' Cristina said with coldly calculated rudeness. 'You have been both insolent and clever, right from the start, when you put yourself so charmingly in Juan's path. It was a pretty ploy. But things haven't gone to well just lately, have they? You have been a little too clever, I think, and a little too insolent. You have over-reached yourself. Your type always does.'

'I don't have the slightest idea what you're talking about,' Paula said stiffly.

'You are transparent,' Cristina said in scorn. 'Your ambition is as visible as a toad behind glass. But I'm afraid your little plans regarding Juan Torres have come to a premature end!'

'You have no right to speak to me like that,' Paula said stiffly, feeling her nerves tingling at the insult. 'I'm not interested in Juan's money.'

'His *money*?' Cristina stared at her for a moment, then laughed, showing beautiful, pearly teeth. 'Is that it? Did you imagine that he was a rich man? A good catch for a little bourgeoise like you?'

'Someone else called me that, last night,' Paula said drily. 'But from the other side of the fence.' Her mind was confused behind her calm expression. 'As for Juan's wealth, if I ever gave it a thought, I just assumed that he was a rich man, though it's hardly relevant. Isn't he?'

'Ah, what a disappointment you're in for,' Cristina said with silky relish at some hidden joke. 'Juan Torres barely has the money to keep Alcamar going. Why do you think he has never had his nose repaired? He has a foolish compunction about making the staff at Alcamar wait for their wages so that he can pay a plastic surgeon. Didn't you know?'

'No,' Paula said blankly.

'You poor goose. You should see your face. Did you have visions of marrying into the Torres fortune?'

'Of course not. But Alcamar—and that beautiful yacht——'

Her eyebrows soared. '*Epoca*? Juan has no money for toys like *Epoca*,' she retorted scornfully. '*Epoca* is mine, girl. As for Alcamar, the land is all put to citrus. There has been a glut of oranges and lemons in the Mediterranean that has ruined thousands of land-owners. Didn't you know that, being such a keen environmentalist? The farmland scarcely pays for its own upkeep. He's planted new orchards of avocadoes and fruit, but it will be ten years before any money comes in from *them*. As for that great castle of a house, how much money do you imagine it costs to keep it staffed and repaired?' She looked amused at Paula's expression. 'There is no Torres fortune, child. The Goyas have been sold to pay the bills, the bank account is empty—and now that his father's Ferrari has been destroyed, Juan Torres does not even have a car!'

Paula stared in horror. All those thousands upon thousands of orange trees planted by Juan, all that back-breaking work—had it all been in vain? Then that was the meaning of the ironic look on his face as he'd stared out over his land from the tower, and said it would have been better if he'd never turned a spade of earth!

'I never even guessed...'

'Did you think Juan started Proyecto Virgen for fun? He needs the money, girl. Without it, he may lose Alcamar!'

'Oh, no!' Paula said in shock.

'Oh, yes. That useless chunk of rock represents all his hopes. He's half-killed himself to plan the project, raise the capital, and keep Alcamar going—and your rabble of so-called nature lovers are trying to ruin him!'

Feeling slightly stunned, Paula thought it over. She'd known very little about Juan, had assumed much. For the first time, she was seeing the true situation, seeing Juan's real position. Far from being born to luxury and wealth, Juan was a man fighting for his home, for his very existence. How frivolous her own concerns seemed now, how much more serious the attack he had suffered appeared in this new light.

Aware that Cristina Colom's sharp eyes followed every expression as it crossed her face, Paula turned away. Silently, she reproached Juan for not telling her about many things. He should have shared his worries with her, instead of letting her just assume that he was hugely rich. He should have told her that behind Alcamar's golden façade, a life-and-death struggle was going on.

It was his pride, she knew instinctively, that had stopped him from telling her. His pride that wouldn't let him be honest with her. That was why he hadn't told her who really owned *Epoca*, too; but she'd rather have made love on the beach, by the sea, than on board this woman's sleek grey toy!

'Yes,' Cristina sneered. 'I thought that would make a difference to your attitude. If Juan were to marry you, he would be sentencing himself to a life of penury. But with my money, he could once again take his place at the very pinnacle of Majorcan society.' Her eyes widened as though she were looking into a brilliant future. 'I would fill that old house with the cream of Europe,' she said softly. 'I would hold balls to dazzle the King himself!'

Paula stayed silent, not trusting herself to reply, and Cristina walked to a chair in the pretty little lounge-area.

She sat, crossing her slim legs, took a cigarette out of a gold case, and lit it. Exhaling a plume of smoke upwards, she considered Paula with narrowed eyes. 'Let me give you some advice,' she said at last, 'whether you are a fool or a schemer, or both. Go home. Now. Forget Juan Torres. It's finished between you. If you go through that door, I can assure you that you will regret it.'

'I can't go without seeing him,' Paula said tiredly.

'Then go in,' Cristina invited with indifference. 'I shall leave you in privacy with him.'

Paula looked up sharply. 'He's awake, isn't he?' she demanded. 'You were lying.'

Cristina shrugged elegantly. But there was silent, malicious laughter in her eyes as she watched Paula open the door to Juan's room.

He was sitting by the window, in a red silk dressing-gown, staring out of the window at the deep blue sky over Palma. He didn't turn as she came in. As she stood in silence, not knowing what to say, where to begin, he broke the silence.

'I heard your voice outside. Why have you come?'

'To see you,' she replied, appalled by the emptiness of his tone. 'To...explain.'

'*Explain?*' He turned his head at last, his expression savage. 'The best thing you can do, Paula, is to keep out of my sight!'

She opened her mouth to speak, but no words came. His face was as hard as a carved mask of granite, the contempt on his mouth as cruel as a blow. She'd seen many passions on that face before, but never one so black and frightening as this.

'I was wrong about you,' he said, very quietly. 'I was a fool.'

'Juan,' she whispered, 'I'm so sorry. If I'd known any of that would happen, I'd have died rather than let you go there—— '

'Spare me the histrionics,' he interrupted, black eyebrows descending ominously. 'This affair was planned— in detail. Was it not?'

She looked down, her eyes flooding with fresh tears. 'Yes. It was planned.'

'And you ask me to believe that you knew nothing about it?' The note in his voice wasn't incredulity. Nor even contempt. It was something that hurt far, far more. It was regret.

'Yes,' she said tearfully, her voice shaking with emotion. 'Yes! I *do* want you to believe that I knew nothing about it. It's the truth. They asked me to get you to the meeting—but Juan, I didn't know why! I trusted them! I thought it would just be a simple debate—— '

'They asked you to get me there,' he repeated drily. 'By whatever means were necessary? Including sex?'

'*No!*'

'Then the sex was your idea?' He was grasping the arms of his seat; under the deep tan, the clenched knuckles showed ivory-pale.

'It wasn't an "idea"! It just happened between us! You know that.'

'I know only that you have made a fool of me,' he said roughly. The physical beauty of his face made the emotion on it all the more obvious; Juan was deeply, bitterly upset; the hurt was deep inside, locked away where she couldn't reach it. 'I can understand that you wanted to strike at me,' he went on icily. 'But why the sex? That has been puzzling me all morning. In the end, I can think of three reasons why you might have done

it. Curiosity, simple cruelty, or just for the fun of it.'
His eyes met hers, empty of any warmth. 'I would prefer
to think that it wasn't the first two. So I shall simply
think that it was for the fun of it.'

'Juan,' she said shakily, 'when you made love to me
that night, that was the first time I'd ever been with a
man. I was a virgin until then.'

He stared at her incredulously for a second, then
laughed harshly in derision. 'You show imagination, at
least.'

'I *was*,' she said, her cheeks turning from white to
scarlet at the pain of his rejection. 'I didn't tell you because I was waiting for a better moment——'

One eyebrow arched. 'A better moment?'

'When we had more time.' She reached out to him.
'Juan—my love—you took my virginity. Would I have
given it to you for the fun of it? Or just to lure you to
that hall?'

'You were no virgin.' The scorn in his voice cut across
her raw nerves like a whip. 'Don't sell yourself short,
querida. You were a skilled and talented lover, and you
gave me much pleasure. But talk of virginity is
laughable.'

'If I gave you pleasure,' she said, trying to fight back
the obstinate tears, 'it's because I love you. But that was
the first time, you *must* believe me——'

'No more lies.' He rose abruptly, and towered over
her almost threateningly. 'Dry your tears, girl. It gives
me no pleasure to see you weep.'

'Why won't you believe me?' she moaned. 'I thought
we m-meant so much to each other...'

His eyes darkened. 'I'm not a fool, Paula. You were
ready for sex that night—you told me so. And no virgin
takes precautions against pregnancy!'

'Oh, Juan...' She'd had a feeling that lie would resurface some time, but not like this! 'I was lying about that——'

'Stop, Paula,' he said tiredly. 'My head hurts too much to listen to your lies.'

'They're not lies! If anything, it's you who've lied to me! You let me think you owned *Epoca*. You should never have taken me there,' she accused him painfully. 'If I'd known it was her boat, I'd never even have stepped aboard.'

'It was you,' he reminded her acidly, 'and not I, who insisted on going aboard.'

'After you led me there!'

'It's a sordid topic,' he said brusquely, brushing it aside.

'Sordid? Yes—to make love to me on another woman's bed!'

He stared into her hot brown eyes. 'Are you lecturing me on morality?' he asked drily.

'Maybe you need it,' she shot back. 'You haven't told me the truth about a lot of things! Why didn't you tell me about your financial position? Why did you let me go on thinking you were rich?'

Anger flared in his eyes, and for a moment she almost thought he would strike her. 'Is that it?' he said savagely. 'The money? Was that your real aim, after all?'

She was so horrified that she could only stare at him. If he was capable of thinking *that*, then there really wasn't any hope, not any more. She turned away from him, twisting her hands together. 'Whatever you may think of me, Juan,' she said, very quietly, 'I'm desperately sorry about what happened last night. To you and to the car. And as for your finances, the only reason I care about them is because they affect you. I'm sorry about that, too. You should have told me.'

'I want neither your apologies nor your sympathy,' he said sharply. 'Keep them both for the next man you try to fool.'

'There will be no next man,' she said quietly. 'You are the fool, Juan, if you don't know that.' She looked at his face, and felt despair wash over her as she registered the cold, hard dislike she saw there. 'Oh, God,' she whispered, 'I'm sorry it had to end like this.'

'It ended last night,' he replied, unmoved by her emotion. 'And believe me, Paula, I do not share your regrets. You mean nothing to me now. Less, even, than I mean to you.'

She found no words to reply, either of entreaty or anger. Her eyes blinded by tears, Paula turned on her heel, and walked out of the room. The door clicked automatically closed behind her, shutting out her hopes, her love, her life.

Cristina was waiting for her, a glitter of real fury in her eyes.

'You little tramp,' she hissed with thin-lipped anger. 'I heard everything. How dared you? On my yacht! In my bed!'

Paula brushed the tears away from her cheeks wearily. 'If you were listening, then you'll have heard that I didn't know *Epoca* was yours.'

Controlling her voice with an effort, Cristina stepped towards Paula. 'You, a virgin? That's a joke!' She bared her teeth. 'I presume choosing *my* yacht and *my* bed was a way of proving your power, girl? I could poison you!'

Looking into the white, animal face, Paula knew it was no figure of speech. 'I meant you no insult,' she said as controlledly as she could. 'It just happened.'

'With you, nothing "just happens",' Cristina said contemptuously. 'By God, I had no idea things had gone this far! Just as well that they have now come to an end.' Paula watched her fighting down her anger as though it were a living beast inside her. 'But everything is finished for you, Paula. He has enjoyed you, and now it is over. Juan Torres is mine, and there is nothing you can do about it now. Nothing.'

'Cristina——'

'Go, before I do something I regret. Go, and hawk your spurious maidenhood elsewhere!'

She walked past Paula as though she didn't even exist, and let herself back into Juan's room.

Suddenly, it was Wednesday. Paula was finding it almost impossible to concentrate on her work at Gomila & Rodriguez—her thoughts were a confused jumble.

It was James who picked up, and on Wednesday evening passed on to her, the news from the hospital—that Juan had been discharged the day after she'd seen him, and was recovering rapidly from the injury.

He settled down beside her on her window-seat, her favourite refuge at the top of the house. 'Why not give him a ring?'

'No.'

'Paula, I don't know what happened between you and Juan on Saturday. Some kind of horrible quarrel, obviously. He put some of the blame for what happened on to you, is that right?' She didn't answer, and he went on, ''But he may feel very differently by now. He may not even remember a thing about it. Cerebral concussion has some very strange effects on people.'

'Yes, I know.'

'He's probably dying to see you.'

Paula stared out of the window at the lemons on the lemon tree, in silence.

'Why don't you go up to Alcamar? Maybe you can put it all right with him?'

'*No*. I can't ever put it right.'

'Don't you think——'

'James, I just want to be alone. Please.'

With a sigh expressive of complete bafflement, James got up and stamped off downstairs to join their parents in front of the television set. He didn't understand. How could he?

Her mood was deeply bitter, a kind of black abyss in which she'd been imprisoned for days, without the slightest inclination to climb out. Since the Ramón Lull affair, she'd been the centre of much concern, both at work and at home. A kind of celebrity had descended on her, and all she wanted was to be left alone, completely alone. It was as though some part of her brain had deliberately gone numb to forget the pain of the things he'd said to her.

You show imagination, at least.

The chilling coldness in those black eyes.

No virgin takes precautions against pregnancy!

Well, damn him. Damn him, and let him be utterly forgotten! What right had he had to treat her so savagely? Yes, he'd been hurt, in many ways. But not by her. And she'd been hurt, too, in a way that he couldn't even guess at.

He and Barry Lear were well matched. Two cold-blooded bastards who cared about nothing but what they wanted. The cruelty of his words was almost unbelievable. That he could even suspect her of such deceit, such lies...

He'd said he'd been wrong about her. Wrong? About *her*? Damn his arrogance! And damn her stupidity. She'd been the one who'd made the mistake. She should have stuck with her first instincts about Juan Torres—that he was a ruthless and cold-blood exploiter.

Let Juan marry Cristina Colom, if money was what he wanted. She would make him a suitable wife—the black-eyed vampire!

Let him build every square inch of Sa Virgen, or let it be relegated to the falcons and the lizards for ever. She was through with Sa Virgen, finished with causes of any kind. From now on, she'd make her own damn mind up about what was wrong and what was right, and let people like Juan and Barry get on with their own wars.

The irony of the situation was almost laughable. It had been Sa Virgen which had brought them together, and Sa Virgen which had wrenched them apart. For a stupid misjudgement, she had lost so much. If only she hadn't been so blind to Barry Lear, Andrés Peraza and Julia Symmonds. If only she'd taken the time out from her golden daydream with Juan to think the whole thing through.

If only...

She was hardly aware of the tears that slid down her cheeks now. The dream had been very brief, but unbearably, luminously sweet. It would haunt her for the rest of her life. She'd been wrong about making love, the way she'd been wrong about a lot of things. It hadn't been the event itself that was an anticlimax. It was the rest of her life that was going to be the anticlimax.

She sat for a long while, thinking of nothing at all, just listening to her heart beat. Then, like drops of water falling into a dark pool, idle thoughts resumed.

Surely one morning he would wake up with the knowledge that she hadn't betrayed him, that she was innocent? He probably knew already. He probably knew she had been as much a victim as he had, but just didn't care.

This was her punishment. Dropping her in this bottomless black hole of loneliness was his way of striking back at her.

Or, more likely, his way of getting rid of her.

Of course. Realisation clawed at her mind. She'd been nothing more than a fly in the ointment for both Juan and Cristina Colom. A not very serious rival for Cristina; a bit on the side that had turned into a nuisance for Juan. Cristina was his real choice, she'd always known that intuitively.

She has beauty, a very large fortune indeed—and she shares your opinion that Alcamar needs a woman's touch.

Well, she finally understood exactly what that cryptic sentence meant. Juan needed her money. He needed it to sustain the burdens that Alcamar imposed on him. All that work he'd done on the land had failed to bring enough money in. And, providentially, along had come Cristina Colom, with her yacht and her vast resources...

And Paula Castle had never been more than a diversion for him, an encumbrance that had to be discarded some time. Ramón Lull had provided a violent but apt opportunity to do exactly that. How easy to turn against her, and refuse to believe in her innocence, when he'd finished with her anyway!

They were born for each other, those two; and she, poor stupid fool that she'd been, had been crushed between them.

She didn't care. It was immaterial to her now. She never wanted to see or hear from him again. When he'd appeared on television last night for a brief interview, Paula had left the room with tingling nerves, unable to be in the same room with even his image.

There had been a lot of Barry Lear in the media, too, skilfully trying to steer public attention towards his cause. Judging by the degree of outrage, however, his plan was backfiring on him.

What was she going to do about him? She should have denounced him on Friday night. But, like a lot of things lately, she'd made the wrong decision. And now, days later, it was far too late to lodge any kind of accusation against him. What evidence was there, anyway? Her word against his. It was futile.

So there he was, a man walking around free who ought to be facing a charge of criminal assault. Paula shook her head, a deep wave of pessimism enveloping her. The world was full of people who ought to be locked up. Come to think of it, it was equally full of locked-up people who ought to be free. Why should she be so concerned about a Barry Lear more or less at large? Why should she do anything at all for Juan Torres? He wouldn't thank her for it.

Somehow she knew that she would never go to the Environmental Group again. How would she ever be able to tell who was guilty among them, who innocent, who was a sincere believer, who a dangerous fanatic? There were a lot of things she was never going to do again.

Memories drifted through her mind. The tower at Alcamar, the smell of those roses bruised by rain. Juan's mouth on hers. The feel of his naked body against hers, his skin like hot silk under her fingers...

She rose from her window-seat stiffly. She'd been horrible to James, and in another week he'd be flying back to London. She'd better go and apologise to him.

The next weeks were going to be rocky ones for her. She'd loved Juan Torres. Not with a schoolgirl's crush, but with the intense passion of one to whom love had come like a thunderbolt.

Well, she'd been warned. It had been some Moorish ghost who'd whispered in her ear, among the ancient stones of Alcamar; love affairs that start like lightning are briefer than a summer's storm.

For her, the storm was over. And now she must face the slow, parching thirst of the aftermath.

Deep inside the desert of her emotions, there was a spring of hope that he would come back to find her, that all could be resolved in a flood of mutual apologies and explanations. At first the spring ran fresh, Paula's heart jumping painfully at each knock on the door or ring of the telephone. But it was never Juan. And, as the days went by, the spring flickered and died.

Nor did she ever do anything about Barry Lear. There was nothing, as far as she knew, that she could do, anyway. Had Juan returned to her, she'd have told him all she knew, would willingly have gone to the police. But, without Juan, she had neither the courage nor the will to go out on a limb alone.

It didn't do her self-respect any good. On the other hand, it didn't expose her to any more misery, either. It was just another unfinished, ugly fragment of the whole useless mess...

Her unhappiness peaked around a week later, when James left for England. Saying goodbye to him at the airport, she felt a wave of such depression wash over her that all she wanted to do was sit down and cry. Under the pretext of buying a paperback for the flight, he led her a little way down the departures hall to be private, and looked down at her pale face fondly.

'You'll find someone else,' he said gently. 'Forget him, Paula. I don't think he'll ever come back.' And when she looked up at him dumbly, he went on, 'I tried to see him last week. Thought I could do a little explaining on your behalf—persuade him that you weren't to blame for what happened. But he wouldn't even speak to me on the phone. I got a very cold reception indeed.'

'Oh,' she said in a small voice.

'Yes. I'm sorry. I know you feel very deeply about him. But he appears to think you were part of the attack on him, and he's a very obstinate man. His mind doesn't change easily. My advice to you is to put Juan Torres behind you, for ever.' He put something into her hand. 'This is for you. A little goodbye present.' He gave her quick hug, then smiled. 'Now, let's get back to Mum and Dad.'

It wasn't until she was in the back of the car, going home with her parents, that Paula opened the flat parcel, and peered inside with blurred eyes.

It was a book. *Setting Up Your Own Home.* And scribbled on the fly-leaf were the words, 'Why not? Love, James.'

Paula looked out of the window, a smile hesitating on her lips for the first time in weeks. Move out of home? Maybe it was about time.

Why not? Why not, indeed?

She started flat-hunting the next week. As she embarked on the long round of reading the papers each night, going to meet prospective landlords, dealing with estate agents, she felt an odd realisation coming over her. Since Juan, she was a different person. Changed in some subtle way.

It was hard to put a finger on it. Maybe 'grown up' was the best way of describing it. More experienced, yes. Less likely to make mistakes. Using her judgement more. Harder, even, as though defensively watching the world for any sign of impending danger.

But also more aware of herself. More aware of her life, her future, and wanting a lot more control over it. She never wanted to be hurt like that again. Never wanted to give another human being the chance to deal out another blow like that.

Nor, she decided quite suddenly, did she want to go on working for Gomila & Rodriguez for the rest of her life. She liked her employers a great deal, and the work was interesting; but she wanted more out of life, and with her talents, she knew she could get more.

And so it followed naturally that, as soon as she was settled into her new flat—in the old quarter of Palma, with a fabulously romantic view over the rooftops—she should send a letter to Eurotrans.

A summons to the big office on the Paseo de Sagrera followed a few days later. The fact that an area manager had flown all the way from Barcelona to interview her was an indication of how seriously the international firm of translators had taken her letter.

The area manager was more than interested. The fact that she had excellent Swedish in addition to German, French, Spanish and English, was a particular point in her favour. He asked her whether she was prepared to travel regularly, at short notice, and anywhere, and when she answered simply, 'Of course,' he offered her a job there and then.

Life, she decided, sitting in the sun outside the *Lonja* after the interview, was like a balloon. When you let the string go, it just drifted along of its own accord. All you had to do was steer it away from the thorns. It was now a month since the Ramón Lull affair, and in that time she'd lost a lover, left home, set up a flat, and got a new job. All she had to do now was find her lost happiness again.

She went back to Gomila & Rodriguez at four, and told a sorrowful but not astonished Señor Gomila that she was going to be giving a month's notice.

'I shall miss you,' he said sadly, and she was so grateful for that 'I' instead of 'we' that she could have hugged the old man. 'Something has happened to you, Paula. Suddenly you are a woman. A little too much sadness in the eyes. A little too few smiles on the lips. But it is time for you to go. Forget about the month's notice,' he nodded. 'Doña Elisabetta will take over from Monday. We'll give you a month's salary instead.' Waving her protests away, he added, 'You've worked hard enough for us. Much too hard. And this dusty old office is no place for a lovely young woman with such talents as yours. Spread your wings.' He made a bird out of his withered hands. 'Fly, little robin. Fly.'

CHAPTER NINE

IN PARIS, at the beginning of June, she knew.

The conference centre was air-conditioned, and the control-room where the translators worked was cool and dim. Sitting in her little studio in front of the microphone all day, translating interminable speeches from Spanish into French—and sometimes, by way of variation, from French back into Spanish again—was oddly like sitting in a cave, chanting some strange outlandish spell that never ended to yourself. When you emerged into the sunlit evening, and walked along the bank of the Seine, you felt your spirit take wings and soar.

On this beautiful afternoon, the so-often-grey river was sparkling with light, and the air, the people, the ancient stones of the city themselves, all seemed to be acting out that not-so-often-true myth that was called 'gay Paris'.

Paula sat on a bench and stared into the river with beautiful hazel eyes. More than one young man passing by hesitated to stare at her wistfully. She was blooming with health; not even a fortnight translating the convoluted speeches of an international civil engineering conference had been able to dull the glow that seemed to surround her.

She'd had her hair cut after all, as soon as she'd arrived in Paris two weeks ago. The hairdresser had done a beautiful job, cutting the thick chestnut locks so that they fell without artifice into the light, natural look that was so fashionable this summer. The style emphasised the elegant bone-structure of her face and the long, graceful sweep of her neck. But she'd cried to see the thick, glossy tresses fall into her lap.

It was almost like watching her innocence cropped and pruned into something more practical, something that would fit in with the way the world really was.

A little too much blooming with health, she thought drily. Why did she have to feel so wonderful? Why was she sitting here wondering whether he would have black eyes or green—instead of thinking about throwing herself into that sparkling river, as so many girls in her position must have thought over the past centuries?

She *did* feel wonderful, at least physically. The only time she didn't feel wonderful was an acute spell of nausea each morning directly after breakfast. The first few mornings of the conference had been almost disastrous. She'd learned to cope by forcing herself to be sick *before* she left the hotel, and not eating anything until noon. That way, she still felt terrible, but at least she didn't throw up all over the console.

She didn't need a doctor to make a diagnosis of her condition. She knew what morning-sickness was.

Really, she'd known, somewhere deep inside, right from the moment they'd lain down to make love on *Epoca*. She'd known it would happen, and yet she'd lied that she was taking precautions.

Why? She'd asked herself that question so many times...

Maybe she'd just wanted his baby. That was probably the most honest answer.

But also because she'd been foolish, completely inexperienced, absurdly romantic, and deeply in love—which were probably the basic reasons that most women fell pregnant by accident.

So call it an accident done on purpose.

The question facing her now was what she was going to do about it.

There were so many people to be considered. Her parents, she had no illusions, were going to take it hard. Despite their unconventional life-style, they were very conventional people, and having their youngest daughter become an unmarried mother was going to be a disaster for them.

James and Helen were going to be upset, too, if only for her sake. They loved her very dearly, and they, too, would see this pregnancy as a catastrophe for her.

Well, wasn't it? In a few months, her newly launched career was going to come to at least a temporary halt, certainly. She couldn't keep on gallivanting around Europe for much longer, still less when the baby arrived. Financially, she wouldn't be too badly off; she had enough to put by to tide her over a year or two off work. But, in all other respects, unmarried motherhood was definitely going to be a lot more difficult than the other kind.

Which brought her to the person who, besides herself, was most concerned.

She'd come to this bench every evening after work for the past two weeks, to sit here and ponder over the same question—should she tell Juan?

It was stupid to keep up her pretence that she hated him. She loved him, perhaps more than she'd ever done; over the past months, her feelings had deepened and matured, as though in absence from him her emotions had been able to clear and purify themselves, like wine standing in a cellar.

But that didn't make the question any easier to answer. What if he were engaged to Cristina Colom? Though it stabbed her heart like a dagger to think it, he might even be married by now. What if he was? What if she went to him and he, thinking it was some new trick, rebuffed her? After all, if he hadn't believed in her virginity, why should he believe that the child was his?

Ah, *that* didn't bear thinking about, either...

Yet how could she not tell him? The child in her womb was his as well as hers. It carried both their genes, a piece of both their existences. She couldn't hide it from him. No matter how he had treated her, or how she had treated him, she owed him that much.

Paula looked down at her own flat tummy. No sign yet, anyway. If anything, she had lost a little weight, her trim ankles and hips testifying to it. She had very little time left, though. This engineering conference was going to come to a conclusion tomorrow, and she would be flying back to Palma at the weekend. She would have to get herself to a doctor when she arrived back, to confirm that she was pregnant, and to register with a hospital for the birth.

And she would also have to break the news to her family.

Poor things, they were going to be horribly shocked.

If she was ever to speak to Juan, then now was the time to do it. She couldn't leave it any later, or she might never do it at all.

How would he react? She closed her eyes, her mind filled with a vision of his face, dark and passionate, with that crooked nose and those brilliant black eyes. He was an impossible man to predict. She could imagine anger or contempt—even, in her dreams, joy; but she knew that the reality would be something completely unexpected.

Once again, that moment came into her thoughts, that instant of pure energy between them when their child had been conceived. A moment of power, of creation; a crux, as though her whole life had been leading up to that point. Everything had been right at that moment, everything had been perfectly aligned. And whatever had been ruined and poisoned since then, nothing could change the overwhelming importance of that moment.

Yes. The decision came to her as she rose from the bench, and slowly walked back up the street towards her hotel. She must tell him. Whatever the consequences, and whether he believed her or not, she must tell Juan Torres that she was going to have his child.

She delayed telling her parents until she'd seen the doctor in Palma. Dr Lopez confirmed that she was pregnant, and on Monday she took an hour off work to go to her first ante-natal examination at the clinic where she'd chosen to have the baby.

In the sudden flurry of preparations for the birth, Paula found a new and deep thrill. There was joy even in the endless paperwork, joy sparkling in the instruments which examined her body and pronounced it fit, joy in sharing her feelings with other expectant mothers.

If only Juan could be with her through this! She felt immeasurably enriched, excited about her baby to the point of wanting to shout it aloud from the tiny balcony of her flat.

Yet she delayed telling her parents, again. She had to go to Juan first, and see the expression in his eyes as she told him.

She'd been given Wednesday afternoon off. That, she decided, was the day she would choose. It was pointless telephoning Alcamar—he probably wouldn't even speak to her. It would be best to just arrive, trusting that he would be there, and see him in person.

It he was out, she would wait. But she would tell him on Wednesday, whatever it took, and whatever happened.

Making the decision was one thing. Preparing to carry it out was quite another. As Wednesday approached, Paula's moods alternated between anxiety and depression until her nerves tightened like violin-strings, and she could almost hear them snap.

It had been nearly three months since she'd seen Juan. The thought of seeing him again, let alone on such an errand, terrified her.

She could hardly hold the steering wheel as she drove along the Esporles road to Alcamar on Wednesday afternoon. Her mind was a complete, awful blank. She had no speeches prepared, not an idea of what she would say to him. Any possible words she turned over in her mind sounded unacceptably trite; above all, she couldn't bear him to laugh in her face. She would have to rely on her brain to come up with the right words when she faced him at last. After all, she'd been translating other peoples' words for years; surely she could find the right way to express her own?

The high grates of Alcamar towered against the blue summer's sky. It was blisteringly hot, and yet her skin was like ice as she got out of the car to ring the bell.

This time she wasn't expected. It was five minutes before the old man came hurrying down the road with the key.

'*Buenas tardes, señorita,*' he beamed, swinging the heavy gates open for her. '*Cómo estás?*'

'*Estoy bien, gracias,*' she nodded. 'Is Don Juan here?'

'Of course! But he is not at the house. You will find him on the *laderas*.' He waved at the hillsides that rose behind the orange groves. Paula looked ruefully at the corrugated landscape of sun-baked hills; an army could hide there, let alone one man.

'Which *laderas*?' she asked helplessly.

'There is a road he always uses.' He gave her Fiesta a glance. 'You should make it in your car, *señorita*—although it's quite bad. I will show you the way.'

Trying to remember his directions, she set off towards the hills. The road, as the old man had predicted, was atrocious, and her little Fiesta was enveloped in clouds of dust as she bounced along.

It took her half an hour to find him, and when she did so, it was purely by accident—she saw the tiny glint of something catching the sun high up among the heather. She stopped the car. A horse was grazing on the hillside, and a little way away was the distant figure of a man. She knew at once that it was Juan. She got out, and with her heart in her throat, started walking up the slope towards him.

The shrill cry of the falcon made her look up after she'd walked a hundred yards. It swooped down over her head, towards Juan, and she saw the big wings spread out momentarily as it settled on his wrist.

That was what he was doing up here, under this vast sky—hawking.

As she got up to him, he was letting the falcon tear at a shred of raw meat from his gloved hand.

'Don't come any closer,' he said quietly. 'You'll frighten her.'

She stopped where she was. The bird was splendid, glossy and fierce, the razor-sharp claws biting into his heavy leather glove. He was leaner and harder than the last time she'd seen him. In the soft leather boots and scuffed buckskin jacket, he looked like a prince in exile. Summer had tanned his skin a deep mahogany, and the loss of weight made him even more stunningly beautiful. She felt her heart ache with a death-pang as she stood in silence, watching him croon to the hawk on his wrist.

Then he lowered his arm slowly, and shook the bird into the air. With an explosive beat of wings that made the horse look up, it surged upwards, arrowing into the sun. She watched it soar until it was just a speck.

'You don't belong in this century,' she said softly.

'Her name is Zahma. She's six months old, and just learning to come back to the glove.' His eyes met hers, jolting her with the intensity of their gaze. 'You look well, Paula.'

'And you.' She'd have given a great deal to be able to just throw her arms around him and kiss him, but she was rooted to the ground.

'They tell me you've been abroad.'

'Paris,' she nodded, and tried to smile. 'It was a very boring job. I'll be in Holland next week. I get around, but all I see is the inside of conference centres.'

He nodded, his eyes assessing her without either warmth or anger. 'When did you have your hair cut?'

'In Paris.' She coloured slightly. 'I won't ask you whether you approve.'

'Whether I approve or not is irrelevant.' He took a small silver hip-flask from his belt and offered it to her. It was Majorcan brandy. The fiery taste brought back intense memories, and it wasn't just the raw spirit that filled her eyes with tears as she drank. She handed it back, not trusting herself to speak.

'So,' he said heavily, 'why have you come here, Paula?'

'I wanted to speak to you.'

He drank in turn, then corked the little flask. 'Is there anything to talk about?' The question wasn't ironic, just matter-of-fact, and that made it cut even deeper.

To hide her pain, she tried to sound relaxed. 'How's your head, by the way?'

'None the worse,' he said briefly. 'The car, unfortunately, was not so resilient. It's been bought by a collector in Germany. He thinks he can restore it.'

'Oh . . . I'm so sorry,' she mourned. 'It was your father's, wasn't it?'

He nodded. 'One of the more absurd things he left me. I loved my father, but everything he left me has just cost money to run. That Ferrari was one of them; Alcamar is another.'

'Juan,' she said, aware of his deep bitterness, 'I didn't have anything to do with what happened that night. You know that now, don't you?'

'That's irrelevant, too,' he replied coldly.

'Not to me!'

'After three months . . .' He shrugged. 'Whatever the rights and wrongs of it, it's ancient history now. The emotions are long dead.'

She'd thought she was past hurt, but the scar in her soul was bleeding again. 'Don't you care whether I conspired against you or not?' she asked miserably. 'Doesn't it mean anything to you that I'm here?'

'Here she comes.' He was looking over her shoulder at the falcon. His voice took on an authoritative note. 'Stand clear.'

She moved away again, and the bird swept by her, swerved in its flight, then soared upwards without landing on the offered glove. 'You're making her nervous,' he said, watching the falcon with dark eyes. 'Take off your hat. And stand absolutely still, please.'

She obeyed, removing the light straw hat she'd worn against the sun. Inside her was that old feeling of despair. She didn't mean a thing to Juan any more. This was the first time they'd been together for three months, and all he cared about was his damned hawk.

Was there any point in telling him about the baby? She felt the tears pricking behind her eyes. She'd wasted her time. Though her feelings for him hadn't changed, his obviously had. They had died, and all that was left was cold ashes.

This time the falcon landed on his wrist, and stooped to her reward of meat. She watched in silence as his lean fingers stroked the bird's body. Then, deftly, he slipped the leather hood over the bird's eyes.

'You were right,' Paula said. 'That is a beautiful sight.'

'I thought you believed hawking was cruel?'

'Hawks kill sparrows all the time,' she said sadly, 'whether they come back to a man's wrist or not.'

'Exactly,' he nodded, still caressing the bird with firm, gentle hands—the way he'd once caressed her naked skin. He was watching her through narrowed eyes, his expression unreadable, forcing her to make all the moves.

'How is Cristina?' she asked, keeping up her conversational tone.

'As ever,' he replied brusquely.

She took a deep breath. 'Are you going to marry her?'

'Yes.'

The word hit her like a blow, and the sun-baked landscape seemed to swim all around her for a moment. Pale as ivory, she put her hat on again, feeling her fingers tremble against the straw. 'I wish you all the best.' She had to force the words out. 'When is the happy date?'

'In the autumn. A few weeks from now.'

'Yes. The summer's nearly over. She must be very happy. I wish you both joy.' She turned away from him, so that he wouldn't see the tears glistening in her eyes, and stared unseeing at the blurred hills of Alcamar. 'There really isn't much point in my staying here, is there?' she said in a voice that couldn't hide her pain.

'Not if it makes you cry,' he said calmly. 'We were once lovers, Paula. Don't imagine that we could ever be friends.'

'No, I don't.' She wiped her cheeks with her wrists. She'd been so determined not to cry this afternoon. He'd conquered that resolution with no trouble at all. The future that faced her was unutterably bleak and lonely.

'Paula...' For the first time, there was a hint of emotion in his voice. 'You are still the most beautiful woman I have ever seen. Is that any consolation?'

'No, Juan.' She turned to face him. 'It's no consolation at all. I'll leave you to your falcon.'

He looked into her eyes for a moment. *'Vaya con Dios,'* he said softly. Go with God.

'You, too,' she nodded, and turned to go.

She had only walked a dozen yards when his voice reached her again.

'Wait.' He came down the hillside to her, tall and lean, moving with that old, magic grace. 'You said you wanted to talk to me. What about?'

She smiled painfully. 'It really doesn't matter now. Goodbye, Juan.'

He watched her with brooding eyes as she made her way through the knee-high heather, down to where her car was parked.

As she got in, she looked up. He was silhouetted against the skyline, a Renaissance prince with his hawk

and his horse. This is how she would always remember
him. She stared long enough to brand the image on her
mind, then started the car, and turned back towards Alcamar, and the road home.

Cala Vibora wasn't ever a safe bay, not even in
midsummer.

As she guided *Sulky Susan* through the needle-sharp
teeth, Paula's face took on an expression of fierce concentration. There was more than herself to consider, now.
But she knew that her days of sailing alone were num-
bered, and today the blue sea and sky had called to her
with an irresistible yearning. This was how it had all
begun, so many months ago, with a yearning to be alone,
away from other people.

The bright reflection of the sea had given her eyes an
intense green light, a colour they normally achieved only
when she was furiously angry. But anger wasn't her
dominant emotion this morning. The sadness she felt
was penetrating, lonely as the gulls high above, desolate
as the sea. Why had she been such a fool as to expect
anything from Juan? And why had she been so shattered to learn that he was going to marry Cristina? She'd
known in her heart that he would, right from the start.
Telling him she was pregnant would have been nothing
short of disastrous.

Even if he'd believed that the child was his, his reaction would have been fury. He'd have offered her
money. He'd maybe even have offered to take the child
from her. She thought of Cristina's contemptuous eyes,
and shuddered.

No. He must never know that she was having his child.
She must face it alone, the way she'd known in her heart
she would have to.

The wind tumbled her short chestnut curls as she set her course between the angle of the wind and the swell of the current. The cliffs had come into view, and she sliced through the white water with a yard to spare on either side. Then she was gliding into the tranquil waters of the bay, hauling down the sail, her slender body moving with the ease of long practice.

This time there was no sleek grey launch in the bay. The crescent of white beach was deserted, and the sandstone cliffs were silent as the grave.

She anchored *Susan* and paddled ashore, the same girl who had come here in the first week of spring—and yet subtly different. Her face had changed, taken on a mature beauty that sadness had had a hand in shaping. The luscious mouth was turned down at the corners, and there was a mistiness in the deep hazel eyes.

She walked along the beach, lost in memories. The image of Juan was so fresh in her mind, the way he'd smiled as she'd spun round to look at him, the way he'd lifted her in his arms to dump her in her dinghy...

High above her, scarcely seeming to move, two falcons hung against the blue sky.

She focused on them with her binoculars; they were young birds, the chicks who'd been born at the end of winter. Already nearly adult, their fierce yellow eyes would be raking the island for mice and lizards.

What was going to happen to Sa Virgen? She hadn't asked him. Since Ramón Lull, the campaign against the development had disintegrated. Almost everyone had been deeply shocked by the violence of that night, and although no one had ever been charged, the movement had been completely discredited.

The Ministry of the Environment had pronounced itself perfectly satisfied with Juan's plans, which had knocked the final nail into the coffin. Suddenly, no one was around to continue the opposition of Proyecto Virgen. It was all over. Barry Lear had gone back to Sardinia, Julia Symmonds was in England; where the others were, she didn't know.

Within a few months, she expected, building would start. Another reason for today's visit. After the birth of her baby, and once the holiday village had been built, she knew she would never come to Sa Virgen again. She hadn't been able to face work, not after yesterday's meeting with Juan, so she'd pleaded sickness, and with no sense of guilt, had gone down to the marina to get *Susan*, and come to Sa Virgen.

Sa Virgen. Another virgin whose virginity would soon be gone forever.

She tackled the cliff-path with as much energy as she thought was safe. Was it her imagination, or was there a new weight in her belly, a presence that hadn't been there before? She would have to be careful; no matter how fit she felt, the doctor had warned her, it wasn't sensible to strain herself.

Still, she was flushed and panting by the time she reached the top.

The view was magnificent. Perhaps they would put it on the brochures, she thought wryly. Perhaps they would build a restaurant here, with a terrace, and a disco...

No. She knew Juan well enough to know that he would never stoop to that. He'd given his word not to despoil Sa Virgen, and he would keep his promise.

She nestled down among the thyme, and focused her binoculars on the gulls wheeling and squabbling below. Gulls were similar enough to humans, aggressive and re-silient, to be able to coexist with them quite happily. Gulls liked tourists, ate their litter. Gulls could cope.

She looked up sharply as something caught her eye. Down below, another yacht was nosing through the entrance of the bay, its scarlet mainsail bellying in the wind.

Paula sighed in frustration. Summertime had its drawbacks, and traffic—both of the wheeled and marine kind—was one of them. She'd so wanted to have Sa Virgen to herself, if only for a few hours. She watched sadly as the yacht steered through the rocks, and drifted up to moor next to *Sulky Susan*. The sail dropped, and she heard the distant splash of an anchor going overboard. There was only one person aboard, a man; and something about the way he moved made her turn the binoculars on him, her heart starting to pound.

She wasn't completely certain until he'd rowed the painter to the beach. The way he strode through the shallows, hauling the boat after him, was unmistakable. Juan!

He'd seen *Susan*. He knew she was here, so it was pointless to try and keep out of his way. Biting her lip hard, Paula sat up among the thyme to watch him. Maybe he wouldn't come up the cliff-path, guessing that she'd be there, and wanting to avoid her. But the dark figure was heading her way with a purposeful stride, and she felt nerves tighten around her heart. Would he be angry with her for coming here? Would he be indifferent? She prayed that at least he'd be kind. She felt too fragile to stand up to any more battering just yet.

But as she watched him approach, five minutes later, her heart sank. She knew that look on his face so well. His brows were black with anger.

He arrived at her clump of thyme like a thundercloud. 'What the hell do you think you're doing?' he demanded tersely. Towering over her, he looked distinctly intimidating. 'You should never have come here alone. This place is dangerous!'

'There was no one to come with me,' she said in a small voice.

His frown eased. 'You're not being very responsible, Paula. People have been killed coming through Cala Vibora. You shouldn't have done it. Not in your condition.'

'My condition?' She looked up at him quickly.

He nodded, his expression heavy. 'Yes. I guessed.'

'How?' she asked quietly.

'Oh, it took a little time to sink in. I may be a fool, but not a complete fool.' He studied her. 'It's written all over you. It shines from your face, as clearly as if you carried a placard saying, "I'm going to have a baby".' He reached out a hand, and helped her to her feet. 'After you'd left, I couldn't stop puzzling over that look. It came to me in the night. I came to find you at work, but you weren't there, and you weren't at home.' He smiled briefly. 'I guessed you'd be playing truant here. As soon as I saw that *Sulky Susan* was gone, I set out after you.'

'I came to say goodbye to Sa Virgen,' she said simply. 'I don't think I'll ever come here again.'

'That would be a pity.' He looked away from her, at the crushed, fragrant thyme where she'd been lying. 'This is almost exactly where we first met, isn't it?' he said in a gentle voice.

'Yes,' she nodded.

'A strange meeting.'

'I suppose you'd call it an unlucky one,' Paula smiled painfully.

'At Alcamar,' he said dreamily, 'there is an old steel crossbow that belonged to one of my ancestors. Once, when I was a boy, I took it down from the wall on a summer's afternoon when no one was looking, and tried it out. It took me all my strength to wind the ratchet.' His eyes turned to her. 'I fired it at a young olive tree in the garden. The bolt split the trunk apart like matchwood. You can still see the scar in the tree now.' She was listening intently, watching his face. 'When I first saw you on Sa Virgen,' he said softly, 'I felt like that olive tree. As though some cruel boy had shot me in the heart with a bolt from a crossbow.'

'Oh, Juan,' she whispered, 'why did you ever turn me away?'

'I was poisoned with bitterness, little one.' Closing his eyes for a moment—his lashes were so thick and long for a man's—he went on, 'I awoke in that hospital, so stunned and confused. You weren't there—but Cristina was at my side, ready to fill my mind with lies and hatred against you. I won't tell you what she said about you,' he said with a wry smile. 'You can imagine the insinuations, the proof, the evidence she had ready. I was vulnerable, still suffering from concussion. By the time she had finished, she had me believing that you were the most evil woman in Spain. When you came to see me that afternoon, I was mad with pain and grief. I thought you'd betrayed me, Paula.' He grimaced. 'It's taken me all these months to understand just how deceived I was. Not until last night, when the image of your face was in my every thought, did I realise at last how cruel and stupid I had been.'

Paula laid a hand over her thudding heart, as if afraid it would burst out of her breast. 'Please tell me,' she said shakily, 'are you really going to marry her?'

'Marry Cristina? No. I lied yesterday.' He took a deep breath. 'I haven't seen her for weeks. You are the only woman I will ever love, Paula. I could never have felt anything for any other.'

'Oh, my love...' Suddenly she was in his arms, feeling his marvellous strength all around her. 'I've missed you so much,' she sobbed. 'I thought I would die without you. That look on your face——'

'Your poor hair,' he said huskily, running his fingers through the rich brown curls. 'Why did you cut it? You must never touch it again, *adorada*. I forbid you to!'

'And you...' Shameless with need, her hands had run up inside his shirt, caressing the hard muscles of his body. 'You've lost weight, my love. You're like a wolf, thin and hungry!'

'I can't sleep or eat,' he confessed with a ragged laugh. 'I need you the way some men need alcohol or drugs. You're in my blood, and I will never be free of you.'

'I never want to be free of you.' Her fingers caressed his face, revelling in the touch of him, his smell. 'You are my life.'

'I've left scars on both of us,' he said quietly. 'Can you ever forgive me?'

'We must forgive each other,' she said with a tearful smile. 'We've been foolish and misled, both of us. They've tried to tear us apart.'

'But now we're together again.' His mouth plundered hers, the hunger of three months' separation making him almost rough in his urgency. '*Dios*, I've wanted you,' he whispered, his mouth against her throat. 'Not a night has gone by without sleeplessness and restless dreams of you...'

'I need you,' she said huskily, her fingers fumbling with his buttons. 'Don't make me wait!'

They sank down among the thyme, lost in the bliss of holding each other again. No kisses seemed to be enough to fill the aching void; no words were necessary, just the moans and whimpers of love that had been denied too long.

There was no need for preliminaries. Their love-making was almost brutally rough, transcended by an intensity that shook Paula to the core, crowned by a release that seemed to involve not just their shuddering bodies, but the sea and the sky, and the lonely isle itself.

As she cried out his name, feeling him deep within her, it was as though all the pain, all the loneliness of these past months was pouring out of her to be dispersed for ever on the clean winds.

They lay locked together for long ages, feeling the infinite peace of togetherness seeping into their souls. As she slowly relaxed, his desire was still hard and urgent inside her, and she looked up at him with laughing, joy-filled eyes, knowing he was ready to do it all over again.

'I'd forgotten what joy was,' she told him tenderly. 'Do you believe that I was a virgin now?'

He buried his face in her hair, his voice soft and rough. 'God forgive me for not believing you. God forgive me for the things I said.'

'Did I really give you so much pleasure that first time?' she asked innocently.

'You make love like an angel—if angels do make love. My sweet one, I had no idea that you were a virgin. If I had known...

'If you'd known,' she repeated, 'would it have made any difference?'

'No. It was perfect.'

'It will always be perfect...'

He was moving inside her again, and there were no more words. This time there were other dimensions to their union, tenderness and desire to please, a sweetness that flooded every corner of her being. The gulls wheeled high above, and the sun poured down honey on the arabesque of their lovemaking.

It was late afternoon when she awoke, cradled in Juan's arms, her naked body warm in the sun. He'd been watching her, and as her eyes fluttered open, he kissed her clinging mouth.

'You've been smiling in your sleep,' he told her. 'I hope our baby has your smile.'

'Are you angry—about the baby, I mean?' She touched his mouth with her fingertips. 'After all, it's my fault I'm pregnant. I lied about taking precautions.'

'How can you take precautions against love?' he laughed softly. 'Though somehow at the time I suspected you were being less than truthful.'

'Did you?'

'Yes. Which makes me just as guilty. Shall I tell you what my inner thought was?'

'Yes!'

'That if we were making a baby that night, then so much the better.'

'That was my thought, too.' She hugged him tightly. 'I want your child so much. It'll be a boy, I know it will.'

'Whatever it is,' he smiled, 'we'd better not wait too much longer to get married.'

'You mean that?'

'I nearly lost you once,' he said seriously. 'I don't intend to ever run that risk again. Will you marry me, Paula?'

She didn't need words to answer him. Her mouth did it for her, and it was a long time before they spoke again. 'God, I need you,' he groaned. 'I'll never get enough of you!'

'I haven't told anyone I'm pregnant yet. Perhaps I won't tell them at all! We'll just announce that we're getting married—and let them guess.'

'They won't have to do much guessing,' he grinned. 'I worked it out last night—you're three months gone. It won't be long before it becomes obvious to everyone.'

'I don't care! But what will you do when I've got a great belly?' she teased. 'You won't be able to make love to me on the cliff-top any more.'

'Oh,' he promised with a glint in his dark eyes, 'we'll think up all sorts of ways and means.'

'Have you really not seen Cristina for months?' she asked him.

'Yes. I made it clear that if I couldn't have you, I didn't want anybody. It took her some time to swallow it, but I think she knows there isn't any hope now.'

'She was hateful to me,' Paula remembered with a grimace. 'Not that I blame her. She found out that we'd made love on her yacht, you see. That was very wrong of us.'

'It wasn't planned,' Juan reminded her. 'Anyway, the fault was mine. I should have told you that *Epoca* wasn't mine. My stupid pride, you see—I was rather enjoying showing you around. I was going to tell you in the cabin. But when you lay down on that bed, and looked up at me with those beautiful eyes, everything went out of my mind except the way I felt about you.'

'I feel sorry for her,' Paula sighed. 'She wanted you very badly.'

'But she knew how I felt about you. I never tried to hide my feelings about you from her. Maybe that was why she hated you so much.'

'Did you ever mean to marry her?'

His eyes met hers. 'No,' he said firmly. 'I never said anything of the sort to her. The pressure was all on her side.'

'She was so confident that her money could buy you.'

'Tell the truth,' he probed. 'That's what you thought, too, isn't it?'

'When Cristina told me how poor you were——' She winced. 'I know how much you love Alcamar. I thought you might marry her for the sake of the estate, to keep from losing it.'

'Is that what Cristina told you?' He grinned, showing beautiful white teeth. 'She exaggerates a little. I may be poor by *her* standards, but then she's one of the richest women in Majorca. I'm not the best catch on the island, Paula, but the farm makes enough to keep going. And when the new orchards start producing, we'll be quite wealthy. There's certainly no question of losing Alcamar.'

'She told me that if you married me, you'd be sentencing yourself to a life of penury,' Paula remembered, pulling a face at the cruel lie. 'I got the impression you were on the brink of bankruptcy!'

'I was—a few years ago,' he admitted. 'When my parents were killed in that accident, they left the estate in a terrible mess. I had to work for years to get it on its feet again—that's when I planted all those orange trees. The collapse of the citrus market didn't help, but I'm surviving it. I have good contacts, and I keep my prices at a sensible level. I can't afford to be extravagant, not yet, anyway. But you won't lack for anything, *querida*.'

'As if anyone who had Alcamar could lack,' she scoffed. 'You are my treasure, Juan. A hovel would do for me—and Alcamar is a palace.'

He kissed her. 'If you want that marble swimming pool, I'll have it built in a month.'

'The *estanque* will do for me,' she laughed. 'And judging by the way you've thrived on swimming in green water, it'll do for our baby as well. What about Proyecto Virgen? When does the building start?'

'It doesn't,' he said succinctly.

'You're not going ahead with it?' she asked in surprise.

'Not any more. No, it wasn't the bottle on the head that changed my mind. I just realised that I didn't want to be rich that badly.' He stared with smoky eyes at the beautiful, wild landscape all around. 'I was crazy ever to think of bringing tourists, strangers, here. Sa Virgen must stay as it is, virgin and lovely. Maybe one day you'll let me build a house on the island—just for us.'

'Let you? The island is yours, my love!'

'No, it's yours.' His eyes met hers. 'It's my wedding present to you. Sa Virgen is yours—that will be in the marriage contract.'

She could only smile at him, her eyes filled with tears.

'We're going to be very happy,' Juan whispered, taking her in his arms.

'Yes,' she nodded. 'We're going to be very happy. For ever.'

The sun was low on the horizon, filling the sky with glory. He held her in his arms, his strength surrounding her. 'I'm not going to leave you Paula,' he promised. 'Not ever again.'

Harlequin Presents®

Coming Next Month

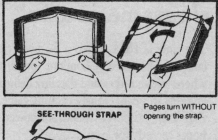
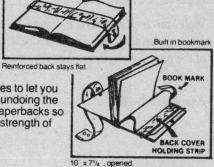

Harlequin Regency Romance™

Romance the way it was *always* meant to be!

The time is 1811, when a Regent Prince rules the empire. The place is London, the glittering capital where rakish dukes and dazzling debutantes scheme and flirt in a dangerously exciting game. Where marriage is the passport to wealth and power, yet every girl hopes secretly for love....

Welcome to Harlequin Regency Romance where reading is an adventure and romance is *not* just a thing of the past! Two delightful books a month.

Available wherever Harlequin Books are sold.